an Angel's Blood

an Angel's Blood

STACEY SCHALLER

L'Dodi
PRESS
OMAHA

ISBN: 978-1-937152-01-7 (paperback - direct version)
ISBN: 978-1-937152-05-5 (paperback - retail version)
ISBN: 978-1-937152-03-1 (Special Edition)

Library of Congress Control Number: 2024922490

L'Dodi Press
3609 Seward St
Omaha, NE 68111
https://ldodipress.com/

(Printed in the USA)

Dedication

In memory of
Hugh McLean
Friend
Mentor
Guiding Light
&
Abby Uecker
Brilliant Starlight
Too Soon Darkened

May You
Rest in Peace

Let's Stand United

Get a Complementary Gift when you connect with us. You'll receive inside info, author's schedule, articles, specials and anything else of interest.

Share It

Let your friends know about *An Angel's Blood*. Find Meme's, Posts and Articles to share.

Table of Contents

What's to Come

Rachel and Mercy quickly scanned their small ready room. In contrast to the main lobby, which was decked to the hilt with the finest amenities the producers could acquire, this room was small and plain. A few photos of Parker and Rene, posing with celebrities who had stood in that very chamber, were nicely distributed throughout the space. A small round table, a couple padded chairs, a tall makeup bench, an overstuffed sofa, and an armoire were the extent of the furniture provided.

"Not much to look at here," Rachel commented with mild bewilderment.

"They must have spent all their decoration budget on the lobby," Mercy observed dryly. Then, her uncertainty reasserting itself, she continued, "So . . . what do we do now?"

Having never been on a talk show—or a show of any kind for that matter—Mercy hadn't known what to expect. Going by the glitz and glamour she'd seen on TV, she halfway expected the entire experience to be something of a red-carpet affair. But she kept reminding herself that, not being an actual celebrity, her treatment wasn't likely to be celebratory either.

"It's not too late. You can still back out of this if you want."

Mercy's color rose to her face. The latent passion burning in her soul dispelled every vestige of reticence.

"But it's important, Mom! The truth—"

A sharp rap on the door interrupted her diatribe. Her last word hung in the air like a murdered thought.

Almost before the duo knew what was happening, Ralph burst in, toting a large basket of balloons and goodies. They were rather taken aback by his abrupt entrance, incredulous at his style, and confounded by his mutterings.

"Here you are, ladies—compliments of the house," Ralph offered awkwardly, thrusting the large wicker vessel toward Rachel. "Uh, hopefully these won't increase your dental bills at all." Then realizing he might have been a bit offensive, he backpedaled. "Uh, not that you need any dental work, of course—"

Rachel interrupted the painful exchange. "It will be fine. Thank you." She smiled graciously as she received the voluminous gift.

Ralph nodded, bowed a little uncertainly, and exited without pomp or circumstance.

Then to distract Mercy, Rachel offered, "Here, sweetheart, why don't you check this out while I find out what we do next?" She handed the basket off to her daughter.

Mercy offered a halfhearted "Sure" and fiddled mindlessly with the basket's contents. She carried it over to the table as her mother peeked out of the room.

A small pink bottle caught her eye. She lifted it from the pile of goodies. It looked like a perfume bottle and was covered with a black top-hat sort of cap. She turned it and caught a glint of the subtle logo on the front.

Lucky You.

Suddenly, she was in another place at other time—

A new bottle of *Lucky You* rested on a teal and seafoam bathroom counter amid a smattering of other teen toiletries—toothpaste, a brush, mousse, and toner. Mercy had just burst in. The bathroom was a typical household bath for a typical middle-class home. Mostly white accented with teal and copper tones, it was as comfortable and relaxing as any ordinary bathroom.

But this was no ordinary situation. Blood was spattered everywhere. Towels stained crimson littered the floor. The tiles were slick with blood and water.

The tub held a panic-stricken girl.

"It won't stop," she cried weakly. "Help me!"

The conversation was interrupted by a knock—not uncommon, as it *was* a doctor's residence. Rachel asked Mercy to get it. Still twirling a fork with a sizable bite of the pasta attached, she sauntered toward the door. She heaved it open then stood there surprised.

The sun was setting low in the distance, painting bright oranges and rich purples across the evening sky. It had darkened enough that the streetlamps came on, and the deep shadows below the trees were murky as midnight.

The figures before her were obscured by the dusk, but Mercy recognized them at once. "Mr. and Mrs. Matthews. How are you?"

Martin and Nancy Matthews were the parents of her good friend Bridget. They stood there, immense uncertainty weighing their expressions. Mercy reached out and gave Nancy a strong hug. Nancy could no longer hold back the tears that stood so close at hand. This undid Mercy, and the floodgates loosened. Martin battled to restrain his own.

"Mercy, are your parents home?"

Having heard a bit of what went on, Clayton and Rachel had come up behind Mercy. Clayton rested a comforting fatherly hand on Mercy's shoulder.

"Nancy, Martin," Rachel greeted them, "What can we do for you?"

Martin was in dead earnest. "Can we talk? We need to know what *really* happened."

Acknowledgments

A good book is never the handiwork of just one person, and everyone who plays a role should get their moment in the spotlight.

This is especially true of *An Angel's Blood*.

Originally penned as a screenplay, this story is the result of the blood, sweat and late nights of a dedicated team of writers, who I want to thank from the bottom of my heart.

I thank Rev. Alvin D. Foote for his irreplaceable contributions, adding unforgettable characters like Ralph, and bringing his extensive EMT experience to the table to help us achieve the realism that is so essential to this tale.

I thank Rachel Burtwhistle, who, though not a writer, provided a mother's heartbeat, and for whom a key character is named. Rachel, thank you for your priceless fingerprint in this story.

I thank my editor, Dori Harrell, for elevating this book to a new level of professionalism.

I thank my sister, Dawn Christiansen, and grandmother, Mildred Brush, for their insightful comments and astute suggestions, helping to make *An Angel's Blood* a compelling read.

I would like to thank my father, Brad Schaller, for his support and encouragement. His contribution put this book into the hands of those who need it most.

I thank the rest of our writing team, who, though preferring to remain anonymous, brought their passion and dedication to the table. Without them, *An Angel's Blood* would merely be a wisp of a dream without their help.

Finally, I would like to thank all the friends and family, too many to name here, who have brought their passion and support to bear, spreading the word and propelling this both to its rightful place of influence in the world.

Author's Note

Why me?

What do I know? What can I offer? Why should I trouble myself to write a story like *An Angel's Blood*?

Fair questions indeed.

But I couldn't *not* write it.

This story is so much bigger than a tale about women's issues or some victory of policy. It's a story about the *human* condition.

It is a story of hope and healing.

So . . .

Who *better* than me?

An Angel's Blood

In my colorful life, I have come to see the humanity in all, to discover the depths to which we each can fall, to feel the hope everyone holds to rise above their failures, and to understand the need in our society for those who *can* to speak for those who *can't*.

That is the heart of *An Angel's Blood*.

My failures in life have become my driving force to lift others who have fallen as well.

Don't despair. There is a future. There is a forward.

And my disappointments in life are my motivation to stand for justice, to help the helpless and defend the defenseless, no matter who or where they are.

Perhaps that is you. Perhaps that is someone you love.

I wish for you to find light and life in these pages.

Stacey Schaller,

> Author of *An Angel's Blood* novel
> Cowriter of *An Angel's Blood* screenplay

CHAPTER ONE
Awakening

Snap!

Breaking twig. Pounding feet.

Running. Ever running.

Crowded woods. Grasping limbs. Rocky path.

"Breathe! Breathe!" she told herself, but breath would not come.

A formless terror pursued. Bearing down with ghostly silence, it threatened to overwhelm her at any moment.

Running harder. Feet like lead.

The path grew longer with every step. Despair filled the air.

She had to reach the end! She must! Mere moments remained. Time would expire.

Muddy nightgown. Treacherous trail. Wet. Cold. Piercing.

An Angel's Blood

Branches clawed like cats. Long hair whipped, tangling in the twigs that clutched at her.

Stumbling. Falling. Into a slippery ditch she tumbled.

Brambles entangled. Thorns jabbed.

She tried to scream. Only silence.

The dark terror was upon her!

She woke with a start. Her heart was pounding like a jackhammer. Wearily, she tried to wipe the fog from her bloodshot eyes.

Cindy looked around the room, struggling to gather her thoughts. Only slowly did she return from the forest of her nightmare.

Despite her throbbing hangover, her vision cleared. The room was unusually messy. Her guest had already gone, but the evidence of his presence lay everywhere. Clothing, dishes, and blankets lay strewn about the room. Two wine glasses rested on her end table.

Memory of the night before came back to her in a rush . . .

The handsome date.

The pleasant dinner.

The invite into her condo for wine.

More wine.

Rolling in the sack.

That part was fuzzy, but she was pretty sure it was fun.

She couldn't remember the guy's name. Not being one to push for a second date, that was no big deal. She was a liberated woman. She was independent, professional, and had no need of a man to take care of her.

Cindy glanced at the alarm clock: 6:15

It was early. Way too early.

She lay back with a groan. The nightmare was always the same.

She tried to push it out of her mind. Rising, she determined to recenter herself. She flipped on the light, half expecting the terror to emerge from the shadows, and stepped over to the mat.

Breathe slowly.

Focus!

She willed her pounding heart to settle into a gentle rhythm and began her first yoga pose.

Pushing forty, Cindy was rather pretty. She was trim and fit and was almost fanatical about eating healthfully. Soy, fat-free, and gluten-free products lined her pantry. Most were the expensive brands.

Cindy liked the finer things. Being single, childless, and well paid, she could afford them. Modern art from the various galleries she supported hung in carefully selected places. Designer furniture sat strategically throughout the apartment.

Notable awards adorned her walls. Photos of celebrities and friends were artfully interspersed with artifacts from her escapades around the world. The townhouse could, in fact, have easily been the set of a magazine photo shoot—except, of course, for the remnants of her sleepover.

As dawn peeked through the window, Cindy finished her yoga routine.

The clock was kissing 7:30 as she added the final touches to her attire. Artful makeup masked the evidence of a restless night. Her golden pixie cut, carefully styled, gave the impression that she was professional, powerful, and *chic*. Her immaculate black pantsuit with white silk blouse lent power and class to her persona. Her stiletto pumps lifted her, literally, to a higher vantage point in the world.

Everything was in its place.

The front door closed behind her. Latte in one hand and attaché in the other, she slid artfully behind the wheel of her Mercedes SL550 roadster and cranked it up. She backed out of the drive and was off. With a bit of a growl, the cardinal-red convertible roared down the road, Cindy behind the wheel, ready to conquer the world.

The morning sun was just peeking through the curtains. It was a typical teen girl's roost. While not a disaster, the artifacts of an active life lay strewn about the room. School books, art supplies, clothing, pictures, and the occasional long-expired food item lay scattered around. Posters of favored music groups hung from the wall. An amoeba-shaped lump covered roughly the middle of the bed, leaving one to make a wild guess about the exact location of the teen buried beneath the blankets.

A beloved old alarm clock ticked off each second. Mechanical leaves fluttered like Rolodex cards, revealing the latest moment in time. One more click and the clock read 7:30.

The door flew open. A pair of little Chinese girls charged excitedly into the room. "Mercy! Get up! Get Up!" the girls shouted.

Full of energy and life, the irrepressible duo pounced on the globulous mass. A muffled moan escaped the besieged teen. Arms shot out from under the blankets, flipping them down to reveal her drowsy features. Blond hair poked from the pillow, like straw.

"Why are you girls up so early?" Mercy groaned.

"You're gonna be on TV today!" Molly, the (slightly) older of the two, announced.

Mercy let out another moan. "Why does it have to be so early!?"

Just then their mother, Rachel, poked her head in.

"All right, girls, let your sister get ready."

The "twins," as they were called (though adopted from different orphanages), stopped bouncing on the bed, clambered down, and darted from the room.

Though chiding, Rachel's tone was warm, and her brown eyes bore the glint of matronly pride in her daughters.

"Good morning, sweetheart. Breakfast in ten."

Mercy groaned sleepily in reply before rising drowsily. She grabbed her towel and headed for the shower.

The welcoming scents of pancakes, bacon, and eggs enticed Mercy as she stepped into the kitchen.

Though clearly dressed for a special event, Mercy still exhibited a style all her own. From the top of her head, crowned with a red knit beret, to the tips of her toes, shod with heeled black leather ankle boots, she was both trendy and conservative. A lacy black tank covered her white satin blouse. Rustling as she moved, her white-and-gray plaid skirt boasted a single bold stripe of brilliant scarlet. In her hand hung a slender silver chain from which dangled a delicate heart pendant.

But her most standout feature was the long black glove she wore on her left arm. Made of lace, the glove extended past her elbow. A scarlet suede bracelet ringed her wrist. From it dangled a single copper medallion engraved with the words "Choose Life."

Rachel's chestnut mane was bobbed and curled just below her shoulders, giving her a classic look. Her homemade apron, practically glowing from the yellow floral print, protected a sharp gray skirt suit as she scurried about to prepare breakfast.

The little girls "helped" Rachel set the table, each clattering dishes and tableware loudly. Molly was orderly and meticulous. Sophie, on the other hand, artistic and fast, placed the items randomly. They loudly disputed their differences of opinion, until Rachel distracted them with more productive pursuits.

The kitchen was comfortably cluttered. As the center of daily life, the kitchen table fielded homework on quiet afternoons and boisterous evenings playing Monopoly, Skip-Bo, or Life. A modicum of dishes nestled on the sink, awaiting their baths, while pots and pans lined the stove, each awaiting its turn to serve delectable dishes.

Amid hanging kitchen trinkets and family photos, nestled a plaque. Arranged so that it could be clearly seen from any vantage point in the room, it read, "Be Strong and Courageous."

The bold green calligraphy evinced the feeling that the words were equally an inviolable command and a hearty invitation.

As Rachel prepared the breakfast and attempted to manage the activities of the twins, West, Mercy's younger brother, ran the griddle. Barely ten, West was the only ginger-headed member of the clan, leading to the family's good-natured teasing that he was the only child in the family who really *was* adopted.

Clayton, known as Dr. Patterson to the rest of the world and as Daddy to the children, labored to work his scarlet tie into a perfect knot.

"You could skip the tie, you know," Rachel quipped as she set a fresh batch of pancakes on the table.

"Can't. I'm the boss. I *have* to wear a tie!"

Rachel giggled and gave him a light affectionate bump as she returned to the stove.

"Mom should be here anytime," Rachel said.

"You know," Clayton responded, shifting mental gears at the sudden change of subject, "I *have* offered to take the day off."

Mercy dove in for a quick hug from her mom.

"Hey, sweetheart," Rachel asked, "are you ready?"

"Umm," Mercy mumbled uncertainly.

"Good morning, Mercy," Clayton added as he put the final touches on the stubborn knot.

"Hey, Dad," she greeted, sidling in to give him a quick hug as well.

"Mom," Mercy asked, lifting her necklace to her mother, "can you help me with this?"

Rachel took it with a smile. "Sure."

Rachel carefully encircled the fine chain around Mercy's slender neck. Then, remembering the other topic from which she'd so suddenly veered, she responded to Clayton. "You know you can't be away today."

"I know," the good doctor replied.

"Mrs. Sinha is due, and you said she could deliver at any time. And Mom doesn't have to be in court today."

She coaxed the minuscule latch into place. Once done, Mercy took her seat at the table, digging into a piping hot pile of pancakes, while Rachel turned her focus back to breakfast preparations.

"Are you sure you two will be all right?" Clayton wondered. "I get nervous about these talk shows."

"It's *Parker and Rene*. What could happen?"

"All the same, some people get pretty testy about what you have to say," Clayton retorted.

"I know."

There was a light rap on the wall next to the kitchen. Everyone glanced up.

"Grandma!"

The younger kids dashed over to give her a hug.

Though watching kids for the morning, Janice Finch, Rachel's mother, looked sharp and professional. Her midnight-blue skirt suit accented her sky-blue eyes and salt-and-pepper hair. She set her attaché down and embraced the swarm of excited children.

An attorney for thirty-nine years, Janice had taken corporate law by storm. She'd been poised to make partner with the high-profile firm Locke, Locke, Blackwell, and Smith a mere four years after hiring on.

Then Rachel had been born.

When Janice had gazed into the eyes of that precious new life, she couldn't imagine giving up priceless moments with Rachel to conquer the high-pressure world of corporate law. Within eight months she had recruited two partners, and they'd struck out on their own just miles from the cold steel towers that had once consumed their lives.

"Good morning, Janice," Clayton said.

"Hey, Mom," Rachel added, "thanks for helping today."

"Anytime," Janice replied. "West, could you run to the car and bring in my file box?"

"Sure!" He dashed for the door.

Janice gave Rachel a squeeze and joined the kids at the table.

"Listen," Rachel offered as she stepped in to help Clayton with his collar, "we plan to be back to the clinic by four. Will you be all right without us?"

"Oh, maybe I can get along without *you* for a bit," he teased. "It's *Mercy* I'm not so sure about."

"Very funny." Rachel wrapped her arms around his neck and planted a light kiss on his lips. "Now get going or you'll be late."

"All right, my love," he replied. He gave her a good squeeze and turned to bid the kids farewell.

"I'll see you all later."

"Bye, Dad!"

The twins rushed in for a final hug.

Heading out the door, he cast one last look toward the kitchen. "Just call if you need anything."

"Of course." Janice smiled.

Sipping hot creamed coffee, Rachel sat beside her mother, listening to the line of questions Janice asked Mercy. Like Clayton, Janice was uncertain about Mercy revealing her story on a talk show and wanted to prepare her for the experience.

A short while later, the clock hit go-time. Rachel and Mercy grabbed their things and headed out.

As the door closed tightly behind them, Mercy couldn't help feeling a knot rise in her stomach. She nervously plopped onto the passenger seat of her mom's Subaru wagon.

Noticing Mercy's tension, Rachel gave her gloved left hand a squeeze. "Be strong and courageous," Rachel gently reminded her.

With a sigh, Mercy unenthusiastically repeated the words. "Be strong and courageous."

The sun hovered over the city like a brilliant golden orb poised on a hazy gray shelf. Parts of the city hadn't yet heard reveille, their streetlights still dispelling the deep darkness of night. Sleepy drivers swarmed onto the roads like ants, as if on cue, dread filled and eager to begin the mundane grind of their daily employment.

An Angel's Blood

The freeway, which just minutes before had offered miles of open road, lay snarled with cars, SUVs, vans, and trucks—each jockeying into position to shave a few moments off their commutes.

Cindy's part of town boasted an easier drive. Upscale—even luxurious—houses lined gracefully curved streets and looked out over artificially beautiful vistas of manicured golf courses, man-made lakes, and curated parks. Most residents—executives, professionals, and millionaires—had long since departed the neighborhood, leaving them nearly bereft of traffic.

To clear her mind, she dialed in her favorite radio station and cranked up the tune. The deep base rhythm vibrated her Mercedes like a drum. The insanely skillful guitarists riffed away any thought of the nightmare that had troubled her that night. The heart-pounding tunes kicked up her adrenaline, getting her psyched up for the day ahead.

Cindy merged onto the three-lane vein that encircled the city. Knowing that, typically, the faster drivers cruised along the center lane, she dodged and darted her way through gaps in the traffic until she found a good spot to roll. And for a couple of exits, she made good time. Then she found herself stuck behind a guy who didn't know what his gas pedal was. Jaunting along in the fast lane, he expressed no intention of passing the driver beside him and clearing the road.

An older Chevy Impala wagon, the burgundy paint was faded and the vinyl woodside panel was aged and peeled beyond recognition. Numerous stickers, signs, and labels made a patchwork of the back of the car.

Cindy thought that a little tailgating might get his attention.

He didn't get the hint.

As the cadre of cars rounded a bend in the freeway, a prominent billboard emerged. It pictured a well-known local businessman, George "Geo" Rayburns, standing next to some "green" vehicles he was selling at his dealership, Rayburns Transportation. The vehicles ranged from compact cars to buses—and all were electric. George's company slogan was painted boldly across the graphic: "Go GREEN with Geo!"

Cindy scowled at the billboard, reacting with utter disdain. She glanced impatiently at the slowpoke in front of her.

One brightly colored bumper sticker caught her attention. It read, "I'm not perfect. Just Forgiven." Beside the words flashed a logo—a painted cross covering a rough, hand-drawn spiral. New Life Community Church.

The color rose suddenly to her cheeks, her fury exploding so quickly, it was breathtaking. She lay on her horn. Other drivers glanced over to see what the commotion was.

No longer willing to wait until the slower driver cleared a path, she gunned the convertible. The three-hundred horses under the hood kicked to life. Her rear wheels complained for a moment, then the car shot forward. Cranking the wheel, she dodged over onto the left shoulder. With her mirror mere millimeters from the median, she flew past the Impala, cut sharply back onto the freeway, and made tracks.

Other drivers honked their disapproval, but Cindy barely noticed. She had to get out of there.

Shaken, she cranked the music even louder.

CHAPTER TWO

Beginnings

The studio nestled in an old-but-chic part of town. Boasting ancient brick factories that had been converted into boutique shops and swank condos, the studio stood out as a center of art and style. A vast mural covered the monumental edifice, recounting that district's days gone by. Historic structures and local celebrities were immortalized in blazing color. Prominently centered over the mural was the logo for the most talked-about talk show since *Ellen*, the *Parker & Rene* show. Flanking each side of the logo were painted busts of the hosts, each recreated so artfully that, if they weren't the size of the building, you'd swear you were looking at the actual people.

Rachel and Mercy found the parking lot to be well packed by the time they arrived. Cast and crew already filled their slots, leaving a few visitors-only spaces near the front entrance. Rachel found a spot, pulled in carefully, and popped the Subaru into Park. The engine sputtered to a halt, and the two overawed ladies wandered toward the lobby door, gazing all the while at the fantastic artwork.

Just as they entered the building, Cindy arrived, shattering the stillness with the music that emanated from her carriage. She parked near the Subaru but left a few spaces in the hope that none would be filled, and her car not be marred by the carelessness of another motorist.

The growl of her engine grumbled to silence. She switched off the radio and took a final glance in the vanity mirror. Everything was still immaculately in its place. She took a deep breath, gathered her thoughts, and slid out of her convertible.

The lobby contrasted sharply from the edifice outside. While the fortress-like exterior celebrated the history of the community, the lobby exalted the modern. Contemporary furniture offered stylish comfort to the waiting guests. The counters of glass and chrome gave the space an elegant feel. The logo, again, hung front and center—this time in 3D relief. The hosts were now immortalized in portraiture more in keeping with their native size. Accompanying them were top-grade images of celebrated guests who had been on the show. Modern art and sculptures adorned the spacious room at various tasteful points. Not being a modern art aficionado, Mercy was clueless about what some of the pieces were, but several looked interesting.

They approached the security desk. Of all of the furniture in the room, this seemed the most mundane. A half-moon shaped kiosk near the middle of the lobby, it sported a Formica countertop and plain white facia. The Parker & Rene logo figured prominently on the facia, but the kiosk was adorned with little else.

The security guard welcomed the pair warmly. "Good morning. How are you today?"

Apparently middle aged—and rather ordinary—he contrasted starkly against the sparkling beauties who waltzed around the studio. His chocolate complexion hid the wrinkles of time, and his tight, close-cropped curls boasted salt-and-pepper tints, leaving one hard pressed to guess his age. But age didn't chill his temperament. One could see he was still light and sprightly and maybe a bit mischievous too. He sported a navy-blue uniform with a gold security badge that announced his rank as lieutenant.

"We're fine," Rachel responded uncertainly. "Um, where do we go? We are guests—"

"Ah. Rachel Patterson?" he responded, lifting a clipboard. "And you must be Mercy."

Mercy smiled politely and nodded.

Rachel brightened. "Yes, that's us."

"I have your guest ID's right here. Please sign in and then Marsha will take you to your ready room."

He slid the clipboard to Rachel and lifted their guest badges toward them. Rachel grabbed the IDs, handing one to Mercy.

They glanced over to see a pretty young intern with perky lips, a clipped smile, and rather unruly wavy brown hair. Marsha waited patiently and attentively for them to be ready. Mercy hung her badge around her neck as Rachel concluded the last swoosh of her signature. As she handed the clipboard back, the intercom beeped, grabbing his attention. He lifted the handset.

"Yes, Ms. Long," he responded. After a brief pause, during which a somewhat shrill but unintelligible voice delivered apparent orders, he replied, "Certainly! I'll take care of that right away," losing not a whisker of cheerfulness in his businesslike tone.

He hung up the handset, smiled at Rachel and Mercy, and stated with finality, "All right. Marsha?"

Marsha smiled and, with a gesture, indicated which way to go. In a moment the trio disappeared down the cavernous hallway and into one of the rooms. Ready rooms gave guests a chance to relax quietly and prepare for the show. They could read, enjoy snacks, practice their presentations, nap—whatever made them comfortable. They also enjoyed privacy, in case they needed to change, and could get their makeup done before hitting the stage.

Moments after their departure, Cindy marched into the lobby. Though a bit older than many who buzzed about the grand space, her studied beauty and upscale style clearly showed that she belonged among these people. As she strode up to the security desk, the intercom buzzed again. The guard again picked it up smartly.

"Yes, Ms. Long?"

Cindy leaned into the counter slightly, offering a subtle hint that she preferred to be helped immediately. The hint was not received.

"No, ma'am," the guard replied to the voice on the other end of the line. "He has not arrived yet."

As far as Cindy could tell, the guard had not even seen her.

"Yes, ma'am. Of course," he continued, busying himself about a couple sheets of paper that had suddenly become vitally important.

Again hinting, Cindy huffed sharply and checked her sparkling-but-delicate Citizen watch. Growing more agitated that he was not comprehending the immediateness of her desire for assistance, she rapped her long, painted fingernails on the countertop.

Somewhat annoyed by her interruption, but still maintaining professionalism, the guard held up his hand, indicating that he would help her in a moment. Her impatience grew more pronounced, irritation covering her countenance like a bad mud mask.

Finally, he terminated the call.

"Good morning," he offered brightly, a hint of mischief in his voice.

"I have been standing here forever!" Cindy retorted coldly, disdain dripping icily from her lips.

Knowing the type, the guard couldn't help tossing in a little verbal jab as he spoke.

"How may I help you, Miss …"

His question trailed off as he waited for her to complete the thought. While in polite conversation one response would be appropriate, the guard was rewarded with a reply more in keeping with what he expected.

"Cindy. Pierce." She enunciated each name, almost as if she expected the guard to be a little slow on the uptake. "You may call me Ms. Pierce."

"Certainly, *Ms.* Pierce," he replied. "Please sign in here."

He offered her the clipboard, which she apparently was familiar with, and slid her guest ID across the counter.

"Here is your ID. Linda will show you to your ready room."

Cindy was irritated by the tête-à-tête, not certain of who had ended with the upper hand. In her world, losing was weakness. There was no room for failure—it didn't matter how small the battle. This was a lesson her father had drilled into her with crushing force, and she didn't dare let herself entertain the notion that a mere rent-a-cop had outdone her.

She heatedly scribbled her signature on the sheet below Rachel's, then barely acknowledging the existence of Linda, she marched toward her ready room.

"Welcome to the *Parker and Rene* show," an artificially deep voice announced to the studio.

A can light suddenly went dark, casting the speaker into cinematic twilight.

The announcer wore a rumpled khaki tweed jacket with brown suede elbow patches, a lime-green tee, faded jeans, and sky-blue penny loafers with white socks. His portly countenance, framed by a blond bed-head hairdo and a ginger goatee, belied a complete lack of seriousness in his demeanor.

He was nonplussed by the change in lighting.

"Today's guests are—"

A sharp voice offstage interrupted his introduction.

"Ralph! Quit messing around! Do you have the baskets in the ready rooms?"

"Oh!" Ralph remembered. "Not yet." He replied as if he'd suddenly been ripped from another dimension via a time warp. He seemed both startled and befuddled by the realization that the task hadn't been done.

The voice was none other than the show's producer, Catherine Long. Middle aged and pretty, she had a no-nonsense air about her. She was sharp, intelligent, and quick on the draw. Dressed in a black long-sleeved tee and black slacks, she almost looked like the female counterpart to Steve Jobs.

Catherine prided herself on being able to meld into the background and remain unnoticed, even if she stepped into camera view. This was handy at times, when she needed to surreptitiously place something on the stage during the show or help escort a guest from the stands while taping. Though most companies relied on interns and low-level help to accomplish these tasks, Catherine was a hands-on producer who knew the pulse of every aspect of her show. She wasn't above doing anything that must be done to make her shows run like clockwork, and audiences rewarded her exceptional diligence with hit after hit in the ratings.

Ralph Graham was the unofficial "court jester" of the production. Every company had one, and Ralph was the beloved thorn in the side of the *Parker & Rene* show. His haphazard way constantly tried the patience of Catherine—and anyone else who loved order and some level of predictability. Ralph was a walking chaos generator, and unexpected disasters would happen everywhere he went.

But Catherine couldn't afford to cut Ralph loose either. As good as he was at creating small disasters, he was better at fixing big ones. Virtually a jack-of-all-trades, he would change lights, fix appliances, salvage hard drives, run cameras, handle errands—anything Catherine needed. More than once he'd rescued an entire episode from oblivion or helped a guest shine on camera.

The only issue was keeping him focused long enough to make it all work.

"The guests are already here," Catherine declared. "Get it done!"

"Yes, Ms. Long." Ralph darted off the stage and out the door, scurrying to complete the task as ordered.

But though he obeyed with admirable speed, he could be heard muttering, "Yes, Ms. Long. Right away, Ms. Long. Humph! 'Slave' is my middle name ..."

Rachel and Mercy quickly scanned their small ready room. In contrast to the main lobby, which was decked to the hilt with the finest amenities the producers could acquire, this room was small and plain. A few photos of Parker and Rene, posing with celebrities who had stood in that very chamber, were nicely distributed throughout the space. A small round table, a couple padded chairs, a tall makeup bench, an overstuffed sofa, and an armoire were the extent of the furniture provided.

"Not much to look at here," Rachel commented with mild bewilderment.

"They must have spent all their decoration budget on the lobby," Mercy observed dryly. Then, her uncertainty reasserting itself, she continued, "So . . . what do we do now?"

Having never been on a talk show—or a show of any kind for that matter—Mercy hadn't known what to expect. Going by the glitz and glamour she'd seen on TV, she halfway expected the entire experience to be something of a red-carpet affair. But she kept reminding herself that, not being an actual celebrity, her treatment wasn't likely to be celebratory either.

"It's not too late. You can still back out of this if you want."

Mercy's color rose to her face. The latent passion burning in her soul dispelled every vestige of reticence.

"But it's important, Mom! The truth—"

A sharp rap on the door interrupted her diatribe. Her last word hung in the air like a murdered thought.

Almost before the duo knew what was happening, Ralph burst in, toting a large basket of balloons and goodies. They were rather taken aback by his abrupt entrance, incredulous at his style, and confounded by his mutterings.

"Here you are, ladies—compliments of the house," Ralph offered awkwardly, thrusting the large wicker vessel toward Rachel. "Uh, hopefully these won't increase your dental bills at all." Then realizing he might have been a bit offensive, he backpedaled. "Uh, not that you need any dental work, of course—"

Rachel interrupted the painful exchange. "It will be fine. Thank you." She smiled graciously as she received the voluminous gift.

Ralph nodded, bowed a little uncertainly, and exited without pomp or circumstance.

Then to distract Mercy, Rachel offered, "Here, sweetheart, why don't you check this out while I find out what we do next?" She handed the basket off to her daughter.

Mercy offered a halfhearted "Sure" and fiddled mindlessly with the basket's contents. She carried it over to the table as her mother peeked out of the room.

A small pink bottle caught her eye. She lifted it from the pile of goodies. It looked like a perfume bottle and was covered with a black top-hat sort of cap. She turned it and caught a glint of the subtle logo on the front.

Lucky You.

Suddenly, she was in another place at other time—

A new bottle of *Lucky You* rested on a teal and seafoam bathroom counter amid a smattering of other teen toiletries—toothpaste, a brush, mousse, and toner. Mercy had just burst in. The bathroom was a typical household bath for a typical middle-class home. Mostly white accented with teal and copper tones, it was as comfortable and relaxing as any ordinary bathroom.

But this was no ordinary situation. Blood was spattered everywhere. Towels stained crimson littered the floor. The tiles were slick with blood and water.

The tub held a panic-stricken girl.

"It won't stop," she cried weakly. "Help me!"

Mercy jumped, startled out of her thoughts, still lost in the world between her memory and her now. Her mother had given a small cry of surprise as Ralph burst in again.

"Oh, I'm sorry, miss. 'Startle' is my middle name." Turning to Mercy, he introduced the woman who'd stepped in with him. "Gena Rose is here to do your makeup."

With Mercy's first glance at Gena Rose, she knew they would get along. It wasn't the goth style—the black leather jacket, the heavy black combat boots, or the black makeup—though that helped. And it wasn't the interesting array of piercings and tattoos, though that didn't hurt. What Mercy saw in that instant was Gena Rose's welcoming smile and genuine openness. There was a sparkle in her eye that said she really cared about people and wanted to do as much good as she could.

Gena Rose had a purple streak in her shoulder-length unnaturally blond hair, and her jewelry jangled with her every motion. She carried a largish canvas bag, which held her mountain of makeup products.

Rachel stepped in behind Gena Rose, who handily took charge of the situation, and observed her work.

"Good morning, Mercy," Gena Rose said with businesslike cheerfulness. "Please have a seat."

"Sure." Mercy moved to the makeup bench.

Gena Rose started right to work, deftly preparing Mercy for her moment before the cameras. Unlike last time, Ralph didn't make his exit. He hovered about Gena Rose, his romantic interest obvious. While she didn't necessarily return the sentiment, she showed remarkable patience toward him and his awkward advances.

"So," Gena Rose began, "what we'll do today is take off all of your makeup and—"

"So, Gena Rose, did you get my call?" Ralph interrupted.

As Gena Rose painted Mercy's face, the conversation rolled along in a strange way. Mercy realized that, though Gena Rose and Ralph were interacting, each was participating in two different conversations.

"Yes," Gena Rose replied with cheerful terseness, without looking away from Mercy. "Once we have done that," Gena Rose continued, turning Mercy in her seat to face the mirror at a particular angle, "we will spray—"

"So, what do you think?" Ralph questioned cluelessly.

"—your hair and—" she pressed on, not missing a beat.

"Does Friday work for you? Friday is my mother's birthday party, and I promised her I'd bring a date this time."

Finally, a bit frustrated, she addressed him. "Ralph, please. I'm working." Then refocusing her attention to Mercy, she carried on. "We're going to highlight your mouth and eyes. Does that work for you?"

 "We'd like just a light, natural look—nothing to make her look older than she is," Rachel interjected,

"I can do that," she cheerfully responded.

Ralph, still on the wings of the conversation, took her to mean something very different. "That's great! So, when can I pick you up?"

Gena Rose rolled her eyes as she fished in her grand bag for the necessary product.

Just then, Catherine poked her head in, obviously hunting for Ralph. When she spied him, she snapped her fingers sharply.

Ralph, familiar with that sound, jumped to attention and whirled toward the doorway.

Catherine shot him a look that would have been deadly had any projectile actually ejected from those smoldering orbs. "Senator Stevens is already here! What are you doing!? Go take care of him!"

Ralph discovered fifth gear and darted out of the room behind Catherine.

"I'm sorry about Ralph," Gena Rose offered. "He's a little weird, but harmless."

Noticing Mercy's sudden tension, she brightly added, "Don't worry about going on stage. Parker and Rene are very nice. You'll do fine."

Rachel had also stiffened on hearing the senator's name.

"Is that Senator *George* Stevens?"

"Of course," Gena Rose replied pleasantly. "He and Parker are great friends. He drops by all the time."

Mercy turned white as a sheet, her stomach churning in Titanic knots.

Oblivious, Gena Rose continued, "So do you want your hair up or down?"

Cindy's ready room matched Mercy's in nearly every detail. Perhaps the furniture was arranged differently, and maybe the cadre of celebrities that graced those walls varied from those featured in Mercy's den. One could not tell, but what one could discern was that no expense was—uh—*made* to deck out the room. A tense, impatient Cindy deposited herself in a stuffed chair, which was neither a La-Z-Boy nor a recliner, and busied herself with work she would otherwise have done at the office.

Her phone rang, interrupting a particularly furious thumb-typing exercise.

"What!?"

The voice on the other side delivered news that was particularly infuriating. "Didn't Carla give you the procedure chart?"

Another murmur from the line elicited a terse list of instructions. Gena Rose entered amid the conversation and, seeing Cindy on the phone, quietly set to work.

"No! No. We deal with these jerks all the time. Don't do anything stupid. Get video. Send the escorts out. Just follow the list! It's not rocket science. Don't call me today. I have a show to do. If you have a problem, *follow the procedures*. They're there for a reason."

Cindy felt like throwing the phone across the room, but she knew she'd need it later. Instead, she slammed it closed like a clam closing instantly on its prey, sealing its doom.

Gena Rose tried to brighten the mood. "So how are we doing today?"

Wearing her frustration on her shirtsleeve and still smarting from the exchange with the security guard, Cindy barked, "What is it with everybody today? Let's just get this done."

Apologetically, Gena Rose guided her to the makeup chair. "Sorry, Ms. Pierce. Please have a seat, and I'll give you a little brighter look."

"My look is fine," Cindy shot back.

Catherine poked in to greet Cindy, and the temperature in the room changed instantly.

"Good morning, Cindy."

"Good morning, Catherine," Cindy gushed. They shared a quick, polite hug before she continued. "It's so good to see you. I've really been looking forward to this show."

While warm, Catherine was all business. It was getting down to the wire, and she had dozens of details to finalize.

"We've got fifteen minutes. Are you all set?"

"Sure! Everything is great! Thanks."

Satisfied that her guests were properly cared for, Catherine turned to exit, found herself face-to-face with the senator's man, and froze. His laser gaze zeroed in on Cindy.

A former CIA agent recruited by Senator Stevens to head his private security team, the senator's man presented an intimidating presence. The girth of his buff arms rivaled Cindy's waist size. His stocky build gave the impression that a wall was striding into the room. He was dressed sharply in a meticulously pressed charcoal-gray wool suit with a white-collared shirt and red power tie. His trouser crease was so sharp that one could slice bread with it. His patent leather shoes boasted a military-class shine. A Glock 17 butt peeked out from behind his jacket, showing just enough to remind passersby that its owner was not to be trifled with.

He stood head and shoulders over the ladies, and a chill settled over the room. Addressing Cindy, he relayed the senator's orders. "The senator wants to see you."

Attempting to wrest some control of the situation back into her own grasp, Cindy deadpanned, "Great. He's just going to have to wait 'till I'm done."

"Make it quick."

He turned on his heel and marched out of the room.

It was clear that all the women present were terrified of him. They shared knowing glances, tacitly expressing the fear each had felt in the encounter.

CHAPTER THREE

On Stage

The set for *Parker & Rene* was spacious and colorful. Broad sweeps of neutral colors were accented by deep greens (Parker's preference) and lively purples (Rene's taste). The stage was reminiscent of shows like *Oprah* and *Ellen*, offering a broad, flat platform with a brief two-step access from the front and wings of the stage. Merely two feet off the floor, the stage gave the audience the feeling that they were part of the show, not merely spectators.

With the theatrical seating, audience members could enjoy a prime view of the hosts and guests from any vantage point in the auditorium. The rows alternated between Kelly-green and royal-purple upholstery. Each spectator enjoyed an armrest with a cup holder and padded woven seats. Every seat also sported a digital voting module that enabled viewers to weigh in on particular issues.

Buttery-soft stuffed leather chairs, upholstered with ivory calf hide, were comfortably arranged about the middle of the stage, while deep-purple carpeting (Rene won that argument) promised luxurious comfort for anyone who traversed it. And the backdrop disguised several hidden points that guests and crew members could use to enter the stage for poignant reveals.

Rows of can lights, dangling from overhead catwalks, cast rainbows of color across the set. Just out of light and camera range, a pair of cue boards hung, each on its own side of the stage. The digital boards flashed messages to the audience. Some shows would use cue boards to incite their audiences to cheer or jeer, applaud or boo. But *Parker & Rene* was a much classier show and only used the signs to invite the spectators to applaud.

While the studio area was colorful, the backstage was markedly stark. Painted matte black, it was designed to not be noticeable. Crew and guests could meld into the shadows, undetectable by the audience until the right moment. As was typical of a backstage area, it had become a receptacle for every odd castoff, unwanted set piece, forgotten prop, and any item set down in a frazzled moment.

Out of view but in easy reach was the "crafts table." This small board offered refreshments to the hurried crew. Guests and cast members frequented the buffet as well. Water, tea, and Cokes, nestled in beds of ice, were packed in coolers under the table, and atop it, tasty hors d'oeuvres lined transparent serving trays.

It was through this gauntlet of food and set clutter that Cindy sauntered. She stopped just at the edge of the shadows along the stage when she noticed Senator Stevens and his man waiting for her.

The senator was a man of refined tastes. His black pinstriped ISAIA suit was custom tailored. His immaculate white Armani French cuff shirt, starched until it could march on its own, brought a sense of old money to the specter. A deep-gray silk tie, with a solid gold stripe in it, and glossy black Prada monk-strap shoes completed his ensemble—all shouting that the senator was on intimate terms with money.

The senator approached her coolly, exuding subtle menace.

"Got a call from the clinic. Have we got a problem?"

Cindy bristled. Like a medieval castle facing off against a foe, she squared her shoulders, trying to evince confidence. "Taken care of."

He took a long look at her, frustration dripping from his gaze.

Senator Stevens was easily twenty years Cindy's senior. His demeanor suggested he was accustomed to getting his way. He neither allowed nor brooked otherwise. The deep canyons of his aged face showed the confusing lines of one who was used to smiling without happiness. Power exercised had carved particular crow's feet at the corners of his eyes. His salty hair, lightly peppered, waved pleasantly across a broad-creased forehead. Every hair—in fact, every stitch—was perfectly in place.

And, as he preferred in his persona, he expected from all matters that were under his control.

But Cindy was a hair out of place.

"Get it right this time," he said—his tone containing pleasantness and ruthlessness.

A low electronic hum emanated from a darkened room as Catherine stepped in, closing a soundproof door behind her.

The control room buzzed like a hive, dutiful crew members scurrying to their positions. A large digital timer counted down to go-time, pouring palpable excitement into the room with each second that ticked away.

If the hosts were the heart of the show, this was the brain. A massive control board, surrounded by dozens of monitors, centered the space. On each, images of empty seats, buzzing crowds, cued pre-rolls, animated titles, and branded overlays flickered and flashed. Buttons of every color lit the surface of the board, some flashing with urgency. Half a dozen crew members sat or paced, each intensely focused on their task. The intense wait was punctuated by moments of frenetic activity. There was a low murmur, as one would comment to another or as some tech would exclaim quietly when confronted with a problem.

Catherine took a seat behind the director, critically reviewing each aspect of the episode that would soon launch. She had the reputation for noticing every detail and wrangling excellence from every element.

The timer ticked down to "20" and flashed.

"We're on in twenty," Catherine shouted. "Positions, everyone!"

A last flurry of activity brought the handful of people into their seats.

The director gave final orders, cueing the camera operators to execute their directives on his mark. "Camera One," he barked, "Come up on the signage. Be ready for the fast zoom."

The view in the Camera One monitor blurred as the operator whipped his camera around and zoomed in on the enormous *Parker & Rene* logo that hung over the backdrop.

"Two," the director continued, "focus on stage left. Catch the entrance."

Operator Two panned his camera over and framed in on the precise point from which Parker would emerge, smiling broadly and waving at the crowd.

"Three. I need a wide shot of the stage. Come full out."

The operator seemed oblivious to the direction. For a few moments, nothing changed.

"Full out! Hustle, people! Let's go!"

This last tirade snapped Operator Three to attention. The view in the monitor was dizzying for a moment as Three located his mark.

"Four. Sweep the audience."

Four meticulously scanned the seats.

The director noticed a particularly picturesque frame. "Stop. There."

The view froze.

"A little to the left."

Four complied.

"Now, tight in. Be ready to pan right across the audience."

Parker and Rene were poised in their positions, ready to enter the stage the moment they were announced. Each had a special entrance near the wings. They would step into view, meet at center stage, banter a bit, then introduce their guests. They'd done it a thousand times. Though filled with the nervous energy every performer wrestled with before a show, both had a practiced calmness and were ready.

The floor manager, counting down the final seconds, whispered, "Five. Four. Three. Two."

He counted down the seconds with his fingers as well. Each host watched him intently, preparing to spring out on cue.

The theme music rolled up, filling the studio with the familiar refrains of the *Parker & Rene* theme. The duo stepped from their hiding places, pacing rapidly to their meeting point. Along the way, they smiled and greeted the audience with the trademark styles each had made famous.

The announcer interjected, almost like the voice of God, "Welcome to the *Parker and Rene* show, with Parker Fleming and Rene Weeks."

The digital sign lit up, and the audience broke into thunderous applause, some hooting and hollering as well. Over the years, Parker and Rene had become a smash hit on the talk show circuit, and fans were ecstatic at the chance to grab a seat in their audience.

Leveraging his pro-ball celebrity status, Parker had launched the show a decade earlier with another now-forgotten host. And while each had shown class and poise, their screen chemistry didn't jive. Audiences thought him to be intelligent and thoughtful, but they'd found her rather jarring, excessively independent, and coolly distant. Only five episodes into the series, she was replaced by another hostess who, though well liked, was something of an airhead who managed to offend an advertiser one too many times. By the third season, Parker was the only constant on the show.

Then came Rene. She'd brought the class, charm, and wit the producers had been searching for. Within weeks the show reached the stratosphere in ratings and rocketed on from there.

But their meteoric rise brought its conflicts as well.

Parker, easily a decade Rene's senior, brought a wealth of experience and business savvy. His connections and friendships landed the show major sponsors, like Johnson & Johnson, Tide, and Ford Motor Company. His acumen, combined with the entertainment experience Catherine brought to the table, had kept the show alive during all the changing faces, and he felt that his brute-force efforts to build audience and wrangle market share made him the primary driver and lead personality of the show.

Rene, on the other hand, brought that sense of down-home heart and inviting warmth that made the show an attractive way for women everywhere to end their busy days. She had class without stuffiness, culture without arrogance. She had quickly become the queen of hearts—more like Diana than Alice—and could genuinely make the case that her presence had single handedly launched the show from an also-ran to a headline feature.

The two had amazing chemistry on screen, and worldwide audiences loved them for it. But offstage, the sparks flew. Both had strong personalities, an amazing sense of showmanship, and the conviction that they personally contributed at least 60 percent of the magic that made the show a hit—and each was unwilling to be trampled by the other. Parker and Rene made a mint—but so did the tabloids.

As Parker paced toward center stage, fans observed his friendly but imposing figure. Head and shoulders above the crowd, he stood at a stratospheric six foot six. His broad shoulders and massive arms threatened to burst from his tailored suit. Parker was bald by choice, which made pinning his age down a tough task, but his closely cropped beard was lightly salted with silver curls.

With a deep-cocoa complexion, Parker could pull of bold styles that his compatriots of fairer tone could not, and today was no different. Sporting an ivory plaid suit with gold pinstriping, he accented the ensemble with a neatly folded silk pocket kerchief in his signature Kelly green. Brown-and-green argyle socks led the eye toward a gigantic pair of hand-made two-tone saddle shoes he'd custom ordered from a cobbler in London. A massive gold Super Bowl ring glinted in the studio lights as he waved his chocolate hand toward the crowd.

Rene was a vision splendor as she glided from her hiding place toward center stage. Once a runway model, her cherry-red stilettos lifted her nearly eye to eye with her humongous counterpart. Scarlet painted lips smiled broadly and warmly at the enthusiastic audience, and her long nails glinted and sparkled as she blew kisses to the crowd.

Rene chose a classic look that highlighted her bold personality. Her silver-gray sleeveless blouse was accented with an exquisite ruby necklace that paired perfectly with her ruby earrings. Her jet-black pencil skirt terminated just above her knees, and the two were separated by a brilliant cherry-red sash. Rene chose the gray blouse because, against her mocha complexion, white was too harsh a contrast, but darker colors, she felt, made her disappear opposite her flamboyant partner. Parker's style naturally grabbed the limelight, and Rene was determined that it would not become the *Parker Fleming Show, with Guest Host Rene Weeks.*

The duo met in the middle and exchanged pleasant greetings, giving each other a warm, professional hug. They found their marks, smiling, as the audience applause died down. With just a few final claps remaining, Parker launched into the introductions.

"Our first guest today is sixteen-year-old author Mercy Patterson, who penned an upcoming release titled *An Angel's Blood.*"

Rene, adding her comments, made them sound natural and spontaneous, though they were, in fact, carefully practiced.

"When I read the book, I was so moved by what Mercy wrote that I knew we simply had to bring her on the show!"

"Talented and ambitious," Parker added, "she is an inspiration to all of us. Few young people take on a big challenge such as writing a book."

"We'll be back," Rene added, "to talk with Miss Patterson right after this break."

After a short beat, Catherine cued up a commercial card for local advertisers, and everyone breathed a sigh of temporary relief—a short lull in the broadcast storm. A local broadcast monitor lit up with silent images of the car lot at Rayburns Transportation. "Geo" stepped into frame as the words "Go Green with Geo!" Flashed on the screen. The next local commercial played as the production crew cued up to go live. One more commercial—a national sponsor—and they'd be back on the air.

Catherine looked over the director's shoulder as he cued the crew to return to the show. Camera One focused on Rene as she welcomed audiences back and resumed the topic.

But the scene was different.

This time she sported a lavender dress with a deep-purple sash. A diamond and amethyst clip glinted on her hair as she finished her welcome statement.

The camera pulled back to reveal the guests while Cindy picked up the main point of the topic.

"A woman's most important choice is the choice she has over her own body," Cindy asserted. "We want to ensure that all women are guaranteed the ability to exercise their rights."

Rene's attire was not the only thing that had changed. As Camera One zoomed out, a slightly different suite of guests graced the stage as well. Gone was Cindy's black pantsuit. In its place was a gray skirt suit with a midnight purple silk scarf. Parker donned a lime-green suit with white penny loafers—his trademark Kelly-green kerchief in his pocket.

Cued by Cindy's remark, Rene took the opportunity to introduce the next guest.

"And this is the perfect moment to introduce our next guest. As a longtime state senator, you may all recognize George Stevens Junior as the leading voice in our state for women's reproductive rights. Please help me welcome Senator Stevens to the stage."

The audience applauded politely as the senator stepped onto the stage. He wore a navy-blue Armani wool suit with a conservative red-and-navy striped silk tie—again, markedly different attire from that which he'd worn before the break. He waved warmly at the friendly audience and paced to his friends, the hosts. He gave each a warm hug and took his place between Parker and Rene, front and center on stage.

Noticeably absent was Mercy.

"Thank you, Senator, for joining us today." Parker's voice barreled deeply, like a young James Earl Jones.

"And thank you for having me," the senator returned. "It's my pleasure."

"Senator," Parker continued, "your new Universal Women's Healthcare Act has been characterized by some as the most important opportunity the state has ever encountered."

Senator Stevens nodded his agreement and launched excitedly into the particulars of the subject. "Statewide, SB-3910 will provide eight hundred million dollars over five years to help women at all income levels have real options in their right to reproductive choice. The allocation ensures that women who could not otherwise afford it are guaranteed access to the care they are constitutionally entitled to."

"But that is not," Rene interjected, careful to maintain parity with Parker's presence in the show, "the only provision of the bill, is it?"

"No. In fact," the senator asserted, "I believe that an essential part of making women's healthcare freely available is protecting women and clinics from the terroristic attacks of right-wing anti-choice extremists."

Cindy added her perspective to the discussion. "We have seen our New Dawn clinics be attacked by radicals that harass the women trying to obtain assistance from us. The new law will create buffer zones that empower us to keep them away."

"We are also," Stevens continued, "cracking down on other anti-choice activities, such as hate crimes perpetrated against those providing women's reproductive services."

Parker took a thoughtful tone. "How will those provisions help?"

"These policies have enabled local law enforcement in other jurisdictions to effectively prevent anti-choice attacks on women," Cindy explained, "and we believe that those policies will be effective here as well."

Providing the journalistic devil's-advocate voice to the discussion, Rene tossed in an objection. "Many of the anti-choice activists insist that abortions continue to be unsafe."

Cindy took up the gauntlet. "You know, of course, that is completely untrue. There are many instances, in fact, where terminating a pregnancy is the safest health option a woman has."

"Why do you think courts require health-of-the-mother provisions in all abortion restrictions?" Stevens asserted. "Sometimes it is the only sensible choice."

A big-screen TV hung over a modern black marble fireplace, the volume turned low. Mercy focused carefully on the screen, hanging on every word.

Mercy wasn't on stage. She sat, instead, on a La-Z-Boy, trying to catch her favorite show without disturbing her grandmother. As the lead partner in her firm, Janice was often free to work from her home office—as many as three days in a week—reviewing cases and discovering evidence in an environment that was free from the busyness and the distractions of the office.

Her home office was appointed as elegantly and as professionally as her office at the firm. Mahogany shelves lined with state and federal statues, West Law journals, and federal form guides, along with Janice's private reading interests, graced both sides of the broad room. The fireplace—more for atmosphere than comfort—glowed warmly with flickering golden flames.

Interspersed about the chamber were numerous artifacts from Janice's many travels. She was active in church and charity and possessed photos of herself with, for instance, Chinese girls rescued from sex slavery and Indian girls rescued from prostitution. She was pictured with a heartfelt farewell banner crafted by smiling Nigerian schoolgirls—many of whom had just learned to read.

But Janice was also photographed with celebrities she'd met through friends or in the course of her work. Chuck Norris, for instance, one of her favorite celebrities, was shown receiving an award granted by a nonprofit she chaired.

The opposite end of the room featured a massive mahogany desk. The ample space it provided was being stretched to its limits by Janice's current case. Folders, briefs, notices, photos, statements, code journals—everything relevant to the case was stacked on or piled next to the desk within easy reach of the determined attorney. The relevant materials crowded tightly around the laptop Janice was working from.

About the center of the room nestled an antique leather sofa. The finely carved Victorian legs upheld a padded leather seat. The supple calf-hide was dyed maroon but had worn in places to more of a pink. The sofa faced the desk, and behind it sat Mercy, so focused on the show before her that the space around her no longer existed.

When Cindy asserted that abortion was safer than giving birth, Mercy exploded. She leaped up and threw a pillow at the TV, exclaiming, "They are lying! Grandma, you know they are lying!"

Janice, startled from deep thought, was a little dazed as she looked up. She slipped the reading glasses from her nose and, twirling them between her fingers, looked keenly in Mercy's direction. "What, darling? I wasn't paying attention."

"I can't believe them! They just—"

Mercy couldn't continue. Collapsing back onto the chair, she burst into a flood of tears. Recognizing her granddaughter's distress, Janice hurried to Mercy's side and wrapped her arms around the sobbing teen. There they sat for some minutes until Mercy calmed down. Though still playing in the background, the show had long been forgotten.

After Mercy had locked down the floodgates of her tears, Janice offered a thought. "Well, maybe *someone* should do something about it."

The special emphasis on "someone" got Mercy's attention. She looked up at her grandmother for a long minute. As realization settled in, she rose up, straightened her dress, and looked firmly into her grandmother's eyes.

"Yes," she announced firmly, then turned and marched determinedly out of the office.

Janice couldn't help a smile of pride and amusement at this beloved young woman.

It was dim in Cindy's office. The nurses and clerks had gone for the night, and most lights were off in New Dawn Women's Clinic. Two lamps lit the sparse room. The first, in the corner, bounced a golden halogen ray off the speckled white drop ceiling, softening the harshness of its brilliance. It had a sort of modern Edison feel to it, at once combining classic industrialism with modern cubism. The brushed steel gave a sort of sanitized medical coldness to the space. The second was a basic brushed-steel desk lamp. The silvery cone shielded the bulb, forcing the beam to cast an oblong disc of light directly on the desk.

The remaining light streamed in as cool—almost green— rays from the marquee across the street. Venetian blinds shrouded the sign from view, but the fluorescent light cast a faint striped glow across the floor and back wall.

The dim glow revealed that Cindy's office exhibited even less of her personal story than did her home. No pictures. No posters. No memorabilia. Not even so much as a book.

The desk, matching the floor lamp, was a unique assembly of steel pipe and smoked glass. All the metal parts were brushed, leaving the impression that it was a long-lost relative of the *Spirit of St. Louis*.

Facing the desk were two black leather office chairs. Stuffed and reasonably comfortable, these pieces looked like cubes with notches cut out. It seemed one might turn them half a dozen ways and still get useful furniture for the trouble. The one notable feature of the chairs was that anyone sitting therein would rest significantly lower than the person behind the desk. Guests would have to look up to their host. This factor was entirely intentional and often gave Cindy sway in a discussion that was not, otherwise, going her way.

Behind the desk was a plush executive chair. Reminiscent of a sports car's bucket seats, the chair was upholstered in jet-black calf hide and double-stitched with white thread. Cindy sat tensely, hunched over the last of the day's paperwork. She had completed most of the forms, arranging them neatly in piles near the corner of her desk. Just a few more reports remained. She clicked away rapidly on the keyboard of her laptop, punching in and verifying the results of her entries.

After a few keystrokes, she scanned the results and winced involuntarily. Frustration cascaded across her tired features. Despite her best efforts, her procedure count was down—and with it, revenue. The protesters that haunted her clinic continued to drive women away, and that was carving deeply into the bottom line.

Her computer "dinged" to inform her of an incoming message. She tabbed over to her email and opened it. The latest poll results showed that SB-3910 held a favorable majority within the state—but just barely. Voters stood 45.7 percent in favor and 43.9 percent opposed, leaving 10.4 percent undecided. The margin was too close to call, but still good news—and it might be enough to sway the remaining three senators who hadn't yet committed to a vote.

Cindy switched back to Excel, and with a couple fast, furious clicks sent the report on its way to the printer. She slapped the laptop closed, shuffled a few pages together, and stuffed them all into her attaché. She rose and reached to turn off the desk lamp.

The phone rang.

A glance at the Caller ID showed that Senator Stevens held the other end of the line. With a ragged, stressed breath, Cindy put on an air of confidence, but her tone came out more petulant than strong. Her irritation and frustration could not be masked. "Yes, sir?"

Cindy paused to let Stevens reply.

"Yes, I did see the numbers," she continued. . . . "Overall, it was favorable." . . . "I really think the bill is going to pass." . . . "Don't worry about the questions. I've—" . . . "Look, I'm taking care of my end!" . . . "It's as good as done. Don't worry."

Cindy hung up as worry crept across her features. The senator was always so demanding, but she wasn't sure this issue could be fixed. She took a deep breath, trying to recall the calming techniques she'd learned in her yoga class.

After a few moments, she exhaled.

Cindy was back in control. Everything would be OK. She was the master of her destiny. She would handle this. It would be OK because she would *make* it OK. Nothing could stop her.

She lifted her attaché, switched off the lamp, and walked to the window to close the blinds. As she stepped past the window, the marquee came into full view.

It belonged to a church across the street. That place was notorious for helping the protesters harass the clinic guests. The extremists would park their cars in that lot and even meet there to coordinate their efforts.

It was New Life Community Church. Cindy froze as the words leaped out at her.

> EVERY LIFE IS SACRED—EVEN THE LIFE OF THE MOTHER.

The panic rose like bile in her throat. Her shaky hand reached for the chain. With a quick motion, she snapped the blinds shut. The signboard disappeared from view. Involuntarily, she clamped her eyes shut, hoping to squint away the message, but like a haunting specter, the words danced before her in the darkness.

CHAPTER FOUR

Misdirection

The crowd sat in polite silence as Rene queried Mercy about her book. Her silver blouse sparkled a little as she moved. Rene held a cup of tea in her hand, from which she sipped as the conversations drew on. Each guest had a little something to drink. It was Catherine's way of helping audiences on the other side of the silver screen feel at home with the show.

Parker relaxed in his chair, his coffee wafting wisps of steam. His right ivory-clad leg was crossed comfortably over his left, and he took a long, thoughtful draught as he listened to the exchange.

"This is quite remarkable," Rene proceeded. "It is unusual for someone your age to become a published author."

"Thank you," Mercy replied.

"You must have had some powerful influences in your life that encouraged you to write. Was that a teacher or mentor of some kind?"

"My grandmother. She always taught me to stand up, do what's right, and let God take care of the rest."

Parker had a thought and leaned forward inquisitively. "I understand that she works in the field of law? Did that help you position the book for publication?"

"Sort of—but not really. She did help me write it though."

Hitting on what he thought to be a relevant point, he added, "So you didn't write the entire book yourself?"

There was a subtle accusation at the edge of his joking tone.

"I did write it. She just helped me be accurate about things, pointed me in the right direction for research, things like that."

"Well, most kids your age won't even write a ten-page term paper. So," Rene wondered, "why a book? What was the driving force behind your work?"

"My friends, peers—anyone my age, actually—really need to take a hard, honest look at the truth behind abortion. It's the locker-room secret. No one really knows what goes on—and the girls who get abortions don't really talk about them. In fact, the only talk there *is* about the issue is the sales pitch in sex-ed class and the gossip that goes on afterward."

The audience muttered their disapproval of Mercy describing it a "sales pitch." Parker and Rene were both taken aback and neither sanctioned her sentiment, but they were entertainment professionals. They quickly restored their composure and resumed the conversation.

"You mentioned research," Rene continued. "What kind of research, exactly, did you do?"

"Really, just what goes on at abortion facilities. I didn't want people discounting me as a nut because I failed to do my homework."

The crowd tittered lightly at the comedy of her comment—mostly because many already viewed her as something of a crackpot.

Rene couldn't help a smidge of a smile. "Many people from a variety of perspectives have weighed in on women's reproductive rights. Why you and why now? What makes your writing different?"

Parker, on the other hand, smarted a bit at the comment. Like most "enlightened" men, he felt that any attack on women's rights was archaic and backward, and he couldn't help challenging this young girl's obviously flawed views.

"Have you actually had an abortion?" Parker asked.

"No."

"So," he pressed, "what qualifies you to write on the subject?"

"Have you had an abortion?"

Parker chuckled, the audience laughing with him. "Not last I checked."

"What qualifies you to do a show on it?"

Parker could see that Mercy had a good handle on debate and good naturedly toned his questioning down. "Touché."

 "The point is that what is true is true," Mercy continued. "If I do my homework, I don't need to personally experience it to be able to write about it intelligently."

"You made some fairly startling statements in your book," Rene inserted, redirecting the conversation. "One of those may be why you actually started writing in the first place. Can you tell us about that?"

A chill settled over Mercy. She sobered quickly, and her expression saddened. The pain was so fresh, she could hardly keep back the tears.

"Well, I had a friend who—" Mercy just couldn't continue. She drew in a shaky breath.

Parker took the cue and stepped in to redirect the conversation. He tried to seem empathetic, but he couldn't entirely hide a condescending edge to his words. "We can see this is hard for you. Losing friends to disagreements over issues can be very painful."

He turned to the audience and continued, "Let's give Mercy a moment to breathe while we introduce our next guest."

Mercy's disagreement with Parker's comment was evident, but she wasn't able to squeeze in a correction before he was on to the next topic.

Rene looked at Parker questioningly. It was entirely uncharacteristic of him to run over a guest like this. In a moment of pain, he was always ready to lean forward, place one of his huge paws on the guest and empathize for a few long moments before moving on. It was good for TV—and it was good for a photo op, if for no other reason. His sense of showmanship was impeccable, yet he so thoroughly blew past this opportunity that it made her head spin.

Being an astute showwoman herself, Rene followed her cue with aplomb. "Please help us welcome to the stage Cindy Pierce."

The cue board lit up, and the audience applauded politely.

Senator Stevens still stood in the shadows nearby as Cindy was introduced. She glanced toward him, catching his eye. A subtle nod, and she turned away. She took a perceptible beat to put on her game face, then stepped out onto the stage. She smiled broadly and waved warmly. An experienced guest, Cindy showed poise and confidence.

 "Ms. Pierce has been our guest numerous times, is an expert on women's reproductive issues and is the director of New Dawn Women's Health Clinics right here in our community."

They met at center stage for a hug.

"Welcome back," Rene offered warmly. "We're so glad to have you."

"Thank you. It's my pleasure."

Parker stepped over for a brief hug as well.

"Cindy," he added, "it's a pleasure to have you with us again."

The applause died down as Cindy took a seat opposite Mercy. It was almost as if they were facing off.

Mercy, horrified, glanced offstage toward her mother. Her stomach twisted in knots, and her heart pounded. Uncertainty burned in her eyes as she looked to her mother for support.

Rachel was surprised and perturbed by the arrival. This hadn't been expected—it wasn't characteristic of this show.

"I am delighted to be here," Cindy gushed. "Any time I can be an advocate for women's rights, I jump at the chance.

"And, sweetheart," she offered to Mercy, "I'm so sorry to hear that you and your friend are not getting along because of this issue. I think that it is such a tragedy when people, particularly young people, are so closed minded to issues that really have their best interests at heart."

Sensing that the conversation was getting off track, Rene intervened. "Cindy, have you had a chance to read Mercy's book, and if so, what are your thoughts?"

"I'm sorry, honey," Cindy responded, her southern heritage emerging a bit, "I haven't. But"—she turned to Mercy—"if I understand correctly, this book is actually anti-choice. Is that right?"

Mercy was uncertain and hesitated slightly as she replied. "Well, not anti-choice—"

"But," Cindy interrupted, "you *do* advocate limiting access to the best options in women's healthcare, right?"

"That's not it—"

"Listen, darling," Cindy offered, hardly giving Mercy time to respond, "you really must be careful not to let closed-minded adults force you to buy into their narrow-minded, puritanical views about sexuality and freedom."

Cindy's statement dripped with condescension. "This country was built on freedom, and these people are trying to take that away from us."

Mercy felt the color rise in her cheeks. The knot in her stomach tightened. She opened her mouth to speak, but Cindy patronizingly pushed forward, rushing into her words with a saccharine sweetness that belied her disdain for Mercy's view.

"Sweetheart, I don't mean any disrespect to your grandmother. I am sure you two are great friends. But does she really know what life is like these days? A lot has changed since she was young, and she really should know better than to push her old-fashioned views onto you. We girls just live in a different world than she did. Once you have lived a little, you will understand what I mean."

Mercy could no longer contain herself. "But why are you pushing *your* views onto *me*?"

"I'm not, darling. I'm simply asking you to allow women to have real choice. Freedom of choice has helped millions of women escape oppression, free them from horribly wrong choices— even save their lives. You would not want to take that away from women, would you?"

"That's not true!"

Rene tried to guide the discussion back toward the book.

"You actually answer Cindy's question in your book, don't you," Rene offered.

"Yes."

"Why do you say it's not true?"

"Because it's just about the money," Mercy asserted. "They don't really care about choice—or the women."

Parker didn't buy Mercy's accusation and tossed his thoughts into the fray.

"You're aware that New Dawn clinics, as well as other women's reproductive care organizations, are *nonprofits*, aren't you?"

"So, you're saying," Mercy countered, "that I could just walk in and get an abortion for free?"

"If you qualify," Cindy replied brightly. "After all, we do have to pay the light bill. But we accept donations, host fundraisers, and give back to the community. Every donation is tax-deductible. How could we be a nonprofit if we only cared about the money?"

"What if the donations didn't come in? Do you stop performing free abortions?"

"Like any charity, we couldn't continue operating without money. That's why we fought for, and won, passage of SB-3910, the Universal Women's Healthcare Act. It guarantees that no woman in this state will ever be denied quality women's reproductive care simply because she can't afford it."

Scattered audience members applauded enthusiastically at Cindy's comment.

Rene picked up the book, the red cover glinting in the spotlight as she flipped to a page she had marked. "Mercy, in your book you assert that clinic counselors 'pressure impressionable young women to make a major life decision without full disclosure, input from their parents, or even reasonable time to think about it.'"

There was an evenness in her tone, like that of a journalist seeking answers, rather than as an activist bulldozing an opponent. Though many in the media confused those roles, Rene took her influential position seriously and was a champion for letting guests speak their own minds, even—or especially—when they disagreed with her opinions.

 "Where did you get your information? On what basis can you make that statement?" Rene asked.

"I did everything in my power to be accurate about what goes on. I interviewed girls, talked with officials, visited—"

Cindy couldn't take it anymore. Offended that this sheltered teen actually considered the anti-choice position to be reasonable, and facing pressure from the senator, she couldn't bear to let Mercy continue speaking. Fire sizzled in her tone—her words practically shooting out like sparks.

"Listen, darling, you have never been to a clinic or received counseling—you have never been in the situation your friends have been in. You do not know the stress—the pressure society puts on them. I am astounded that you would allow the prejudiced views of the patriarchal establishment to color your viewpoint of an issue you can't possibly understand. *You* be pregnant, alone, and scared and see what *you* do. You have no place to judge!"

"I am not judging. I—"

"But you are. You are telling me that you have a right to dictate what I do with my body—and you don't."

"Since when are we 'free' to kill innocent human beings?"

The interchange was heated—the type of theatrics more suited for *Jerry Springer* than *Parker & Rene*. Things were getting out of hand. The hosts shared a glance, then Parker reined in the discussion.

"Mercy," Parker asked, his voice cool and even, "you get into some medically based discussion of women's reproductive health in your book. I wonder, did you ever get involved with a medical professional—say, shadow a doctor for a day—to learn what you discussed in your book, or was it more along the lines of online research?"

"You may not be aware, but both of my parents are medical professionals—"

Mercy, book bag slung over her shoulder, stepped up to the clinic door. Dressed in her sky-blue nurse smock, she was ready for work. As always, the long black glove graced her left arm, and ringing her wrist was the ever-present red pro-life bracelet. Her long, flowing blond hair was tied neatly into a bun, making her look several years older than her actual fifteen years. Her comfortable white Dr. Scholl's scuffed a little as she stopped to pull the handle. Through the large plate-glass window, she could see the Jones children playing with the colorful toys.

It was an unassuming storefront nestled among other equally mundane locations. Situated like a sidewalk shopping center, the Valley Medical Plaza was an ideal location for an OBGYN practice—especially one that provided affordable and pro bono prenatal care to many of the city's low-income families. A plain one-color vinyl sign, plastered to the large storefront window, was the sole indication of the existence of the Patterson Clinic.

Dr. Clayton Patterson was the lead obstetrician, the owner and the founder of the clinic. Short of Rachel and the children, this was his passion. He could work a ten-hour day, slide his feet under the covers, get beeped for a delivery, and spend two more hours watching a new little life squirm and screech her way into the world. Dr. Patterson loved serving the community and had a regular flow of mothers, children, medical colleagues, and community leaders who called on his time. Rachel served with him as well, working hard to create a homey, welcoming environment for the mothers who graced her establishment.

In fact, aside from the inviting accoutrements, like hot coffee and fresh pie, the Patterson's lovey-dovey way with each other was always the talk of the office. They were often invited to "get a room" or "go get married or something." It was always in good nature, and the staff were comforted by the fact that, after years of marriage, these two were obviously not going anywhere. The clinic would be around a long time.

Children loved going to see "the baby doctor." A fun area with bright colors invited the little ones to play, and the nurses always had a treat and a smile for each enthusiastic little bitty. But their favorite feature of the clinic was Mercy. She was the light of the room. Mothers exiting a stressful round of examinations were always greeted by peals of laughter as their children played with Mercy.

Mrs. Jones was very pregnant and flipped through a magazine while she awaited her appointment. Other guests waited as well. A bright couple, the Schmidts, sat glowing in their anticipation. They were newly married, and this was their first. Martha was far enough along that she was asking Rachel for shopping tips. A couple of older ladies, Sally Kronk and Gretta Garfield, quietly shared local gossip. They were members of the same quilting club and just happened to have appointments on the same day. And Nancy Arnold—an independent career woman in her mid-twenties—was just starting to show.

Nancy was single, and as the craziness of pregnancy began to settle in, the "I don't need a man" attitude had crumbled into midnight tears and ice cream. The overwhelming reality of motherhood weighed on her. She came more often than most women, not because there was a problem but because Rachel was motherly and understanding and helped to make the future seem less unbearable.

At a glance, Mercy knew them all. This was her place. These were her people.

Mercy was greeted by the guests as she entered. Mrs. Jones's little ones hadn't noticed her yet, or they would have dashed over and inundated her with their delight. Janie, six and a little bossy, was insisting that Jackson, four and incredulous, play shopkeeper quietly. He was supposed to sit in the chair and wait for her to finish shopping so he could ring up her toy groceries on the play cash register. Jackson, however, was convinced that the little toy fire truck with the ringing bell would be more fun, and he was doing his best to convince Janie of that fact.

Mercy headed over to check out what the kids were doing.

Looking up from the magazine, Mrs. Jones greeted her. "Hey, Mercy."

"Hey, Mrs. Jones! How's the baby?"

"We'll find out in a minute, but everything seems great so far."

"I'm so glad for you. You have such a beautiful family."

"Thank you, honey. You're so kind."

Mercy knelt beside Janie and engaged with her. The kids finally noticed, each coming over and throwing their arms around her neck in a crazy kid-ball hug.

Rachel appeared at the front counter, case folder in hand. She glanced up and noticed Mercy with the kids.

"Hey, Mercy," Rachel called out, "can you come here real quick?"

"Sure, Mom." Mercy rose and untangled from laughing kids. "I'm sure everything will be OK," she offered Mrs. Jones comfortingly as she headed for the nurses' station.

Mercy stepped behind the counter and slid her bag to the floor.

"How was school?"

"Better," Mercy responded. "I'm starting to get a new normal."

Rachel gave her a quick hug. "I know, darling. It's hard."

After a bit of a pause to let the comforting words sink in, Rachel continued in a more businesslike tone. "Listen, when Mrs. Jones comes back for her ultrasound, would you mind watching Janie and Jackson for a bit?"

"Sure!" Her mother's asking was only a formality. Both knew that Mercy loved those kids and would be delighted to keep them entertained.

"Here's some paperwork to file, and could you prep the clipboards for the next appointments?"

"Mm-hmm." Mercy accepted the tasks cheerfully. Concern swept suddenly across her eyes, "Mom, is the baby OK?"

"This time, yes. Everything is going great."

"I'm so glad to hear that." Mercy exhaled, relieved.

Mrs. Jones followed Rachel back into the ultrasound room.

The screen on the ultrasound machine flashed different odd spots of colors as Rachel set it up. With the expectant mother on the examination bed, Rachel whisked through each prep step rapidly and efficiently. She remembered how cold it was to have her belly exposed to the chilly room and how icy the gel felt, so she liked her ladies to be as comfortable as possible.

But short of delivery, this moment was her favorite of all. This was where she got to see those squirming little babies before anyone else on earth laid their eyes on them. Each one was unique. Some squirmed and twisted like acrobats. Others lay quietly, sucking their thumbs. Some kicked or punched. Others fidgeted with their toes. Some had hair. Some even strongly resembled their dads. Rachel could get a good guess of how the child would be from what it would do during the exam.

Mrs. Jones was ready for the gel. Rachel applied it, then quickly slipped the probe onto the clear icy goo.

"This might be a little cold."

"It's fine," Mrs. Jones offered, anxious to see how her little one was doing.

"Good. OK. Here we go."

Rachel fiddled with the probe and adjusted the focus nob until an energetic little figure showed crystal clear on the screen. "That's one active little guy."

"Mm-hmm," Mrs. Jones agreed. Her tone suggested that she, through various bumps and bruises, was well acquainted with the baby's activities.

Rachel smiled broadly. This little guy was a delight. He definitely had his dad's broad shoulders and thick, tightly curled hair.

"Precious little thing. Let's get your measurements."

Rachel stretched thin lines across the screen in various directions, and the calculations seemed magically to appear on the screen. "There. That's good," Rachel muttered, deeply focused on her task. "That's good. OK, now, calm down just a minute for Aunt Rachel. Good!"

Mrs. Jones marveled at how quickly Rachel took the measurements and appreciated how thorough she was. After a couple miscarriages, she was always on edge about how the baby was doing. Visiting the Pattersons always put her mind at ease.

"Oh, look. We know what the sex is. Would you like to know?"

"Absolutely!"

"Well, Mrs. Jones. You have a handsome little boy."

"Blessed be!"

Some tears of joy eked their way out of Mrs. Jones's eyes.

The intercom at the nurses' station beeped.

"Oh! I've got to get that," Mercy told the kids.

She dashed over to answer it, Jackson still dangling from her shoulders. She hit the Intercom button. "Yes?"

"Can you bring the kids back?" Rachel's tinny voice crackled through the line. "They will want to see this."

"Sure!"

Mercy hurried the kids into the room. Their eyes widened as they saw their mom on the bed, huge belly bare, while Rachel rolled the probe.

"Come here and take a look at your little brother," Rachel said.

The kids dashed over. The image of an active little infant appeared on the monitor. He twisted and turned playfully as the children watched.

Janie giggled. "He's squirmy!"

They all laughed lightly.

"He sure is," Rachel replied.

"Mommy? Can we take him home?" Jackson asked, "I want a brother now."

"We sure can, baby. But he's got to stay in my tummy for a little bit longer."

"Awww." Jackson pouted. He crossed his arms in a huff.

Janie edged close to the ultrasound monitor. The little guy was squirming around, twisting and spinning like an Olympic swimmer. She reached out and gently touched the monitor. It was an Instagram moment that brought a tear to Mercy's eye.

"He's so little," Janie said, almost in a whisper.

Dishes dinged, pots perked, and skillets sizzled as the Patterson clan prepared for supper. There was a happy buzz about the kitchen. As Rachel slid the lasagna from the oven, Mercy sliced the last pieces of bread, and Sophie placed the plates and cups on the table.

"Do you want any of these toasted?" Mercy asked her mother.

"Four, probably. You know how your father likes it."

Rachel sliced the lasagna as she gave Sophie further instructions. "Sophie, can you set the forks on please? And there is salad dressing in the fridge."

A heavy rustling, punctuated by occasional grunts and groans, sounded from the living room. After a particularly heavy grunt, Rachel rolled her eyes and shook her head in amusement. The two men of the house were heavily engaged in a wrestling match. And neither, as of yet, held the upper hand—though that probably was because Clayton wasn't trying hard. West practically had him pinned as the scents of garlic cheese bread, Italian spices, and chocolate cake wafted through the house.

"I smell that," Clayton called from the living room.

"Then you'd better get in here before I eat it all," Rachel deadpanned.

Rachel pulled the garlic cheesy bread from the oven and elbowed the oven door closed. It popped shut with a slam. She set the bread and lasagna on the table.

"I want some too," West shouted.

"You know your father," Rachel called back. "If he beats you to the table, you might not get any."

After more grunts and a flurry of activity, two tussled bodies slid into the kitchen on stocking feet. West dashed into his seat. But instead of trying to beat his son to the table, Clayton grabbed Rachel and twirled her around, spinning her into his arms.

"All right, little lady," he said with a mock western drawl, "I want a peck o' that sugar."

Rachel replied, with a coy drawl of her own, "Why, sir, I'm fresh out."

They both kissed, then giggled at the silliness.

"You two are crazy," Mercy said as she took her seat.

"Someday you'll be crazy like us," her father replied.

"Can't wait," she said dryly, drawing a silly grin from her dad.

He rubbed her head teasingly, gave her an affectionate squeeze, and took his seat.

Rachel hollered up the stairs. "Molly! Supper's ready."

Rachel placed the platter, stacked tall with delicious nine-grain bread lathered in butter and sprinkled with garlic, on the table. Finally, the rest of the family was seated.

"Dad, did you read Mrs. Jones's chart?" Mercy wondered.

"Yes, I did. I'm very happy with it."

"It's about time the Jones's got good news," Rachel added.

"I know," Clayton agreed. The crew seemed to be settling, so he asked, "Everyone ready?"

Everyone clasped hands and Clayton began the blessing. "Dear Father, we thank you for all your blessings, your provision, and most of all, we thank you for life—each day, each moment we have to be a blessing to others. In the name of your Son and our Savior, Jesus. Amen."

"Amen," the rest responded.

There was a flurry of activity as each piled their plate with the delectable delights that topped the table.

"Molly, Sophie, hand me your plates," their father directed. Two plates wandered his way, and he filled them with the rich, gooey strands of mozzarella-encased lasagna.

"I wonder what they'll name him," Mercy questioned.

"Who?" West hadn't been in on the events of the day.

"The Joneses' new baby," Rachel replied.

"He's born?" West asked.

"West, your plate," Clayton interjected.

West handed his plate to his father.

"No, not yet," Rachel continued.

"We just found out today that the baby is a boy," Mercy added. She turned to Rachel as an idea struck her. "Do you think I can get something for the baby?"

It was finally Rachel's turn to be served.

"Would you like some?" Clayton asked.

"Of course. Just a little though. I'm watching my figure."

"Yea," Clayton teased. "I'm watching it too."

Rachel rolled her eyes again but giggled. Then, she was back on topic. "I don't see why not. I think Mrs. Jones would appreciate it."

"I saw a precious onesie in the store. I think that would look cute on him."

The conversation was interrupted by a knock—not uncommon, as it *was* a doctor's residence. Rachel asked Mercy to get it. Still twirling a fork with a sizable bite of the pasta attached, she sauntered toward the door. She heaved it open then stood there surprised.

The sun was setting low in the distance, painting bright oranges and rich purples across the evening sky. It had darkened enough that the streetlamps came on, and the deep shadows below the trees were murky as midnight.

The figures before her were obscured by the dusk, but Mercy recognized them at once. "Mr. and Mrs. Matthews. How are you?"

Martin and Nancy Matthews were the parents of her good friend Bridget. They stood there, immense uncertainty weighing their expressions. Mercy reached out and gave

Nancy a strong hug. Nancy could no longer hold back the tears that stood so close at hand. This undid Mercy, and the floodgates loosened. Martin battled to restrain his own.

"Mercy, are your parents home?"

Having heard a bit of what went on, Clayton and Rachel had come up behind Mercy. Clayton rested a comforting fatherly hand on Mercy's shoulder.

"Nancy, Martin," Rachel greeted them, "What can we do for you?"

Martin was in dead earnest. "Can we talk? We need to know what *really* happened."

CHAPTER FIVE

Engagement

The can lights bore down on the stage with piercing heat. Beads of sweat mounted on Mercy's forehead. Glowing in the blinding brilliance, her scarlet beret felt like an oven. Her black glove soaked up the glare, making her arm feel prickly and itchy.

Cindy, also unused to the heat of the spotlight, felt a trickle of perspiration run down the small of her back. It tickled, but she didn't dare acknowledge it. That would, she believed, project weakness and uncertainty.

The conversation was growing heated, each side sniping at the other with increasing devastation. The two hosts were barely able to hold the reins of the discussion. The crowd was becoming polarized, some definitely on Mercy's side, while others wholly agreed with Cindy. As each landed a blow, mixed murmurs emanated from the audience and things were getting lively.

Trying to dilute the sensationalism of the discussion, Rene shot for clarity. "So, Mercy, you assert that abortion should never be legal under any circumstances?"

"That's right. I can't understand how anyone, after seeing what I see every day, could even *dream* of hurting one of those precious little ones."

Some audience members cheered or clapped. Others booed or shook their heads in response. Mercy was beginning to resonate with some, but most remained unconvinced.

Crew members in the control room exchanged glances. Used to Catherine's heartwarming, nonconfrontational shows, they were unsettled by the turn of the conversation. Catherine, in particular, was keeping a vigilant eye for a good moment to cut to a commercial. She was unused to her sets getting out of control, being reputed in the industry for productions more like *Dr. Phil* or *Oprah* than *Jerry Springer*—shows that drew a classy audience and classier advertisers. She knew exactly what worked for each brand and was punctilious about making sure *that* was what happened—every episode.

 "Let's set aside the fact that banning choice would be a major affront to women's rights," Cindy continued. "What about children who will grow up in poverty?"

"You have no crystal ball," Mercy retorted. "You don't know what kind of life a child will have. What right do you have to steal a child's life away just because you think she *might* have a hard time?"

In other parts of the facility, staff were gathering by twos or threes, glued to monitors that played the meltdown in real time.

"As I said," Mercy replied, "my dad is a general practitioner and obstetrician. He takes care of a *lot* of women and their health issues. You could bring *him* on the show and ask, but there are absolutely no health conditions any woman may face that *require* an induced abortion. None! Even if a woman *must* have an emergency hysterectomy, an induced abortion is more dangerous than the operation."

Gena Rose sat against a wall behind the stage, glued to the monitor that the floor manager used to time the segments. The discussion intrigued her. She'd never considered—or even heard—the arguments Mercy made. While she wholeheartedly agreed with Cindy philosophically—as any sensible person would—she had taken a liking to Mercy and silently cheered her on.

"What if a woman's life was in danger?" Parker added, just a slight string of tension edging his cool tone. "Constitutionally, abortion *must* be available for women whose lives are in jeopardy."

Unlike the others, Ralph was rather heedless of the argument at hand. Though keeping quiet (having been threatened on pain of death against making a racket), he wasn't particularly concerned with the topic. He'd donned a headset through which key crew members could communicate with him and was, at this particular moment, delivering snacks and bottled water to a few famished stagehands. With cameras rolling, they usually had nothing to do but to complain and eat.

As Ralph passed through the backstage access, he spied Gena Rose sitting, entranced by the screen. All thought of delivering the goodies slipped from his mind. He walked toward her, still trying to maintain his (near) silence.

"What about children that are unwanted and will be abused?" Rene asked.

"Millions of children, even wanted ones, are abused—despite the availability of abortion. Really, I can't imagine any *worse* kind of child abuse than abortion."

"So," Cindy indignantly interrogated, "you would relegate a woman to have to suffer with a child she can't deal with, no matter what? What if she was raped? Do you want her to live every day with the reminder of a horrible life event?"

"I feel for those women. I really do, but—"

"But you don't understand them."

"No, but—"

Careful not to disrupt Gena Rose, Ralph sidled up and sat on the chair next to her. Without realizing it, he depressed the Broadcast switch on his headset. It was a feature that allowed the floor manager to call for a general evacuation in case of emergency. The audio would play over the sound system throughout the building. It wouldn't go over the air, of course, but everyone in the building would be able to hear what was said.

Cindy's voice took an insistent, almost demanding tone. "You have never experienced their pain, but you feel free to pontificate about their life choices?"

Beginning to whither under the barrage, Mercy desperately reached for an argument that would sail through Cindy's interruptions.

Rene was horrified. Though thoroughly pro-choice herself, bulldozing a teen on live television was not an event she permitted on her show, but the interchange had heated so quickly that she couldn't squeeze in a word—not to mention that she was at a loss as to what to say.

Mercy squealed, "You're talking about stealing the—"

"A rapist pushes his way into a girl's life, and you say she *must* live with the consequences!"

There was a forceful finality in her last words. The pro-abortion audience was on its feet, clapping, cheering, and hooting.

Unwilling to be outdone, a pro-life audience member stood up and shouted, "Kill the rapist, not the baby!"

Pandemonium erupted. Claps and catcalls, boos and whistles rang out everywhere. The show was going crazy.

Out of nowhere, a voice carried through the loudspeakers. "So, what are you wearing to the party?"

It was Ralph.

A hush fell over the bewildered crowd. Everyone looked around, trying to figure out where the comment had come from.

In the control room, Catherine practically vaulted from her chair. "Who was that? Get their mic shut down! Now!"

The sound tech shrugged. Nothing had come through his board.

Ralph, just as befuddled as the silent audience, looked to the monitor. The camera held tight on Cindy and Mercy. Having spoken the words himself, he didn't know what brought the show to a standstill. Now his attention was focused on the guests.

Gena Rose, however, was the only one *not* looking at the monitor. She looked smolderingly at Ralph.

Grabbing the opportunity to regain control, Cindy announced, "It's not a baby. It's a fetus."

Still unaware he was broadcasting, Ralph retorted, "Isn't *fetus* just Latin for 'baby'?"

Half the room burst into laughter and cheering.

Flustered by the entire segment, Rene interjected, "On that note, now might be a great time for a commercial. We'll be right back."

With a flurry of motion, the director ordered a cut to commercial.

The screen rolled out a national ad as Catherine threw up her hands in disgust. "I'm gonna kill him!" She ripped off her headset and charged out of the production booth.

Red-faced and humiliated, Cindy excused herself from the set and headed backstage for the break.

Cindy strode down the hallway toward her ready room, steaming over how the show was going. With the adrenaline wearing off, she was shaky and had begun to reflect on the argument. The whole scene was still a bit foggy in her mind, but she realized that her effort to guide the debate had derailed. She hadn't been able to hold the audience to the end of the logic. And she'd been embarrassed.

Ralph, having seen Catherine charge through the backstage area like a raging bull, darted up the hallway in a safer direction. As he rushed through, he accidentally bumped shoulders with Cindy, shaking her out of her reverie.

Recognizing Ralph, she ordered, "You! Get me some water."

"Yes, miss. Right away," Ralph responded.

"Don't—"

Heedless of her additional volley, Ralph scurried away, intent on getting beyond Catherine's clutches.

"—call me *miss*!" Cindy continued, deflating.

She darted through the door and slumped into an out-of-the-way makeup chair tucked into a quiet corner. Now exhausted, she sighed heavily. She continued replaying the segment in her mind, wondering where she could have gone wrong. The audience was tracking with her, so how did she lose them? If it weren't for some nut on his headset, she'd have won the day.

Ralph reappeared with two water bottles.

"Did you want Refreshing Spring or Spring Clear? Some people say they taste different. I can't tell, but they look different, and maybe that has something to do with it—"

Irritated and distracted, Cindy snapped, "Just give me one!"

"Yes, ma'am."

Ralph reached one of the bottles out to her, but just as she went to grab it, he changed his mind, pulled it back, and handed her the other.

She yanked it from his grasp. "Good grief!" she snarled. "What is it with you people!?"

As Ralph rushed off to cover some other task, Cindy popped the lid and took a sip. Swirling the water around in her parched mouth, she leaned her head back on the headrest and sighed.

Heart pounding. Leaves murmuring. Limbs grasping.

Cindy ran frantically—desperately. The darkness overwhelmed.

The path pricked. Pain seared through her body.

A distant voice. Crying. Terrified.

A young girl called out in fear.

A dark horror—like a panther—pursued.

Cindy cried out. Desperately. Earnestly.

She reached out, but the girl remained beyond her grasp— beyond her sight.

The hounding terror rumbled behind her. It seemed to leap.

The girl screamed.

A crushing paw pressed her shoulder.

With a startled cry, Cindy snapped out of her slumber. Senator Stevens's heavy hand rested on her shoulder. She looked up into his steel eyes.

The senator's boogieman flanked him, arms crossed threateningly.

"The show has been disappointing today."

"Well," Cindy retorted, "the little snot has an answer for everything. We should just hand her the keys to the kingdom and we'd all be in utopia by now."

"Utopia or no, if she continues to run the conversation as she is, it *won't* be utopia for *us.*"

"I've got it all under control," Cindy asserted.

"Now that the bill has passed, we are not going to lose in the last inning, right?" The senator's eyebrows tightened.

"Oh, so now we're scoring by innings?" she quipped, sarcasm dripping from her lips.

The senator's voice hardened. "*I* didn't take the call. *I* didn't mess this up. I won't let *your* messes to become *my* messes."

His steel eyes turned icy. His long gaze telegraphed implications that Cindy wasn't willing to consider. She squirmed in her seat.

"I know you'll do the right thing," the senator continued.

Cindy's face reddened in anger, but she bit her tongue.

Ralph poked his head in the door.

"We'll be on in *one* minute."

The senator, steely eyes glued to Cindy, replied, "She'll be there."

He and his goon slipped out the door, disappearing into the shadows.

Cindy took a long breath, slowed her heart rate, checked the mirror, and put on her game face. After a few moments to get her mind reframed, she headed back toward the stage.

Cindy took a seat as the final countdown to go live began. The tension was still palpable, but things had cooled significantly. Almost like donning an overcoat, she put on her poise.

Mercy, on the other hand, seemed more reticent and deflated as she sat opposite her opponent.

Catherine took her seat, eyes glued to the monitors. She had dealt with the minor disaster and hoped the new session would present a tone much more in keeping with the zeitgeist of the show. The last commercial rolled up on the monitor.

Bright images of smiling professional women greeted viewers as each spoke of her experience with women's healthcare at New Dawn Women's Clinics.

"If I have questions—"

"If I need advice I can trust—"

"If everything else has failed me—"

A soothing, gentle voice followed. "For over thirty years, New Dawn Women's Clinic has offered confidential, reliable advice about women's health. Protect yourself. Our compassionate counselors can walk you through any women's health concern you may have. Call New Dawn today."

The director yelled, "Cut!"

A phone rang.

Cindy slipped it from her pocket. She was no longer on the set of *Parker & Rene*. She stood, instead, behind a film director who was in the middle of shooting the commercial. It was time for a reset.

Cindy checked the number, rolled her eyes, and slipped away. Once outside the film set, she answered the phone with a terse, irritated tone. "What?"

She paused to listen. Her responses were short, and her alarm grew as the conversation continued.

"What happened!?" . . . "It's not my fault." . . . "What did you do?" . . . "We'll never get by—". . . "I know you are—" . . . "I just can't believe this. I don't want any part—" . . .

"But—" . . . "Yes, sir." . . . "I'll take care of it." . . . "No. No. I do understand."

Cindy's irritation collapsed into resignation. "Yes, sir. Consider it done."

She ended the call, visibly shaken and breathless. Bad had gone to worse, piling it all in her lap. And the senator was not someone you refused.

She took a long breath, trying to settle her mind. Once calm, she turned to reenter the commercial shoot. Her eye caught the marquee from the church across the street. This time the marquee read:

> TWO WRONGS DON'T MAKE A RIGHT, BUT CHRIST CAN RIGHT ANY WRONG.

Cindy rubbed her tired, flaming face as if trying to scrub away any memory of the unwanted message.

Senator Stevens flipped his phone closed and slipped it back into the pocket of his iron-gray pinstripe Kiton three-piece. The plush seat in the back of his Cadillac limousine gave him no comfort in that moment. Through his open window, his steel eyes gazed out toward a church.

The limestone steeple stood tall on the city skyline. Huge stained-glass windows, framed with arched oak panes, stood abreast a line of formidable, ancient oak doors. A somber crowd milled about the entrance of the grand sacred ground.

The senator tapped the back of the driver's seat. The chauffeur popped the carriage into gear and pulled gracefully away. As the limo disappeared from view, a procession of saddened guests ambled through the receiving line that graced the church's doors.

It was a funeral.

Mercy stepped out of the door, still clutching her handkerchief. Her eyes were swollen and red from much crying, and she'd donned a black-and gray-outfit, complete with a black knit beret, to show her grief. Her signature lace glove dangled with a silver friendship bracelet. Notably missing was the red pro-life charm bracelet. Janice followed, close behind, equally displaying her grief—though, as an attorney, she was much more practiced at subduing her emotions.

Martin and Nancy stood next to the pastor, receiving condolences from family and friends. Traces of tears stood on their cheeks, but at the moment, their expressions showed more shock than sorrow.

Mercy stepped up to Nancy, wrapping her arms around her best friend's mother. They held each other in a long, strong embrace. Tears did not come, for each had already exhausted herself with weeping.

"I am so sorry," Janice offered after some long moments.

"Where did we go wrong? Why would she kill herself?" Nancy agonized.

Mercy stepped back in surprise. Her face twisted in concern, and she shook her head vehemently. "Mrs. Matthews," Mercy asserted, "that's not what happened."

Nearby, a suited guest, having overheard the conversation, pulled his phone from his pocket. He clicked away at the keys, hammering out a brief, cryptic message.

"We have a problem." He tapped Send and clicked his phone to sleep, slipping it into his pocket as he turned to leave.

It was the senator's man.

CHAPTER SIX
Pressure

The senator and his man edged the shadows backstage. The goon glanced at his phone, then whispered something to the senator. The senator gave a slight nod.

The senator's man scanned the audience for a particular face. Seated among the crowd was one who would be more a part of the show than of the audience—a plant. At last their eyes met. The goon nodded, and the plant took his meaning.

Everything was set.

As the floor manager launched into his countdown, everyone took their seats and settled down for the next segment. There was a buzz about the crowd. Excitement pulsed like electricity through the audience.

Catherine tensed as the seconds ticked off, hoping this round would be more informational than inflammatory.

The red numbers flashed on the countdown clock.

Five.

Four.

Three.

Two.

The On-Air light clicked on. A red light on a camera lit up.

Cropped tightly, the shot focused only on Parker as he looked directly into the lens, addressing a breathless television audience. "Welcome back to today's show. For those joining us late, we have two guests with us today."

The camera light flashed as a red lamp on another camera powered up. The second camera framed in on the guests as he introduced them.

"The first," Parker contributed, "is Mercy Patterson, the author of *An Angel's Blood*, and Cindy Pierce, director of the New Dawn Women's Clinics."

Rene added, "We are discussing the issue of women's reproductive rights. Ladies, thank you for joining us."

While each of the guests acknowledged the welcome graciously, gone were the smiles and warm wishes of the earlier segments.

Parker launched right into the topic.

"So, Cindy, we've enjoyed a spirited discussion so far."

Cindy laughed lightly, brightening.

"Much seems to have been made by anti-choice activists," Parker continued, "about the safety of women's reproductive services. What is your take on the question?"

"I'm very glad you asked, Parker," Cindy offered cheerily. "Surgical abortion is one of the safest types of medical procedures done today. Complications from having a first-trimester aspiration abortion are considerably less frequent and less serious than those associated with giving birth."

Mercy bristled. "How is it possible that an invasive medical procedure is safer than when a woman's body does what it was designed to do naturally?"

"Darling"—condescension dripped from Cindy's voice—"I guess you *haven't* done your homework."

Rene, hoping to keep a balanced tone in the discussion, offered, "Doesn't the CDC publish statistics?"

"Yes, it does, in fact," Cindy replied, "but a more complete statistical analysis is provided by the Alan Guttmacher Institute. Repeated studies released by AGI note the minuscule number of complications from the abortion procedures compared to the incidence of risk and injury to the mother. For instance, about one in four births necessitate emergency C-section procedures. Fewer than two percent of women who chose to terminate their pregnancies report any complications."

"That's a factor of twelve to one," Parker asserted.

"Certainly," Cindy agreed. "Really, when you boil it down, why would anyone choose to undergo such a dangerous event as childbirth unless they were absolutely certain that they wanted that child?"

Mercy was incredulous. "What? That's not even possible!"

"So, you have statistics to counter Cindy's?" Rene asked.

"In some ways, yes. But many of the consequences of abortion are never tabulated. The statisticians aren't even asking the questions," Mercy replied.

"Big words for such a little lady," Parker jabbed.

"Many of the live birth statistics, for instance, factor in procedures performed solely for liability reasons that have nothing to do with the mother's risk factors."

Suddenly, Parker seemed to turn from host to opponent, and he leveled off rapid-fire critiques at Mercy. "And you would know this how?"

"My dad is an obstetrician."

"So, you know this by osmosis?"

"No. I work with him. I know—"

"And you gained your medical degree where?"

"I don't need a medical degree to read medical journals," Mercy shot back.

Trying to rein in the machine-gun dialog and steer the show back on track, Rene interjected, "How has your experience qualified—"

Heedless of Rene's hints, Parker plunged on, cutting Rene off midsentence. "So, you can understand all of the medical jargon they use and actually be able to read it—even though you have not finished high school?"

"I *have* a dictionary—and I know how to use it."

The audience tittered a little at the quip.

"Besides," Mercy continued, "if the dictionary does not have the right info, my dad's medical library does—oh, and there is the *Internet*," she tossed in sarcastically.

"Listen, girly," Cindy threw in. "I have a degree as an RN and fifteen years of experience in the medical profession. Women's health issues have been my life. You have been studying this issue for, what? One, maybe two years? I've seen it all. I know what women go through, and I can assure you, abortion is by far the safest way to deal with a pregnancy."

"What about—"

"Shouldn't medical experience count for something?" Parker countered.

"Any medical procedure," Cindy added, "has some risk, but of all medical procedures that could be performed, abortion procedures are by far the safest."

With a surreptitious glance at the senator and his man, the plant rose from her seat. She was young and somewhat chic, but not standout. Her red hair waved its way past her shoulders, while a pair of sunglasses nestled in her hair, ready at a moment's need. She wore a short-sleeved denim jacket over an ivory sun dress. She had a decidedly "everywoman" look about her.

She threw her line toward Mercy with a compassionate, accusatory tone, slightly tinged with righteous indignation. "What about the back-alley coat-hanger procedures? Would you suggest that women be left with that as their only option?"

Some of the crowd clapped or cheered in agreement.

Parker, seeming to play more the role of an interrogator than a host, took the opportunity to press in harder. "Very good question. Is that your position, Mercy?"

"No," she insisted, "but—"

"Then," he interrupted, "you think there is some room for medically safe abortion care?"

"There's no such thing!"

Again, Rene tried to modify the conversation with a pointed, but fair, question. "Mercy, what would you advocate for—"

Again, Parker bulldozed right through.

"It's kind of one or the other. If you don't allow safe, clinical procedures, women will have no choice but to rely on back-alley hacks."

"Or," Mercy fired back hotly, "they could deliver a live human being!"

"You know," Cindy shot back, "your parents were off by a mile when they named you. If you truly were a person of mercy and compassion, you would not be so heartless toward the women who face such difficult choices."

"Please, ladies," Rene desperately interjected, "let's get—"

Parker pressed on as if Rene wasn't there, shooting questions like a WWII gunner. Joining with Cindy, he'd switched into full gang-up mode. Rene was livid. She shot a withering, frustrated look at him while he continued obtusely.

"How can you consider your position compassionate when you leave so many women hanging out to dry? Do you not believe in freedom of choice?"

"What about the baby's choice?!"

Rene, though most definitely not pro-life, began to side with strongly with Mercy. "That's a good—"

"Honestly," Cindy pressed in, her righteous anger mounting, "did you get your information from qualified medical sources or from those cheesy, badly written anti-choice websites? Some of those people couldn't spell their name if it was written in the dictionary."

"I hardly trust stats from a group like Guttmacher that makes their *living* from killing innocent children."

Mercy's jab was too much for Cindy, and her blood boiled. Her professional, in-control demeanor crumbled away.

Rene, fighting to give Mercy a chance to speak, offered "How did you arrive—"

"So, you have become a doctorate-level researcher?" Parker interjected.

Before Mercy could shoot back, Cindy could no longer contain herself. "Perhaps your mother should have considered our services and saved the world from one more heartless hack!"

The shocked audience fell into dead silence. You could have heard a pin drop.

It was a comment they'd expect from a show like *Jerry Springer*, but on *Parker & Rene*, such chilling clashes between guests never happened.

Mercy's jaw dropped. Scattered audience members covered their mouths incredulously. No one knew what to do. The blow was simply too shocking.

The heat rose in Mercy's cheeks. Steaming tears crowded her eyes. With as much dignity as she could muster, Mercy rose from her chair and rushed from the stage, burying her scorched face in her hands.

Cindy realized instantly that she'd gone too far, but she had no idea how to back away from her cruel comment. From deep inside, an old fear welled up, nearly sending her into a panic. With a couple of deep breaths, Cindy calmed herself and took an air of defiance.

Everyone, hosts included, seemed frozen in time.

Catherine suddenly snapped out of the collective trance. "Bring up the logo. Go to commercial! Get it up! Now, people!"

The switch operator brought up the logo to break and punched up the next commercial.

As the On-Air light cut out, everyone found their minds. The audience buzzed like a beehive. Parker rose and strode off the stage, Rene chasing after him. Rachel, livid at the interchange, dashed backstage to find her crushed daughter.

Cindy glanced toward the side stage and caught a glimpse of the senator. She put on a face of smug satisfaction, hoping to get some modicum of approval from the hard man. Instead, his eyes narrowed, and he shook his head slightly in disapproval. She wasn't surprised but was certainly disappointed and frustrated.

Parker grabbed Gatorade from the craft table, ripped off the lid, and took a swig, when Rene caught up to him.

She was white with fury. "What in the world was that?"

"What are you talking about?" Parker countered nonchalantly.

"This show? We *never* have a show like this! You bulldozed that poor little girl—*and* kept cutting me off!"

"I'm just hosting a show. What is your problem?"

"This isn't *Jerry Springer.*"

"But it *is* my show. If you don't like it, the door isn't locked. Otherwise, you follow my lead."

"We invited her here. We should at least give her a fair chance."

"We'll talk about this later," Parker offered dismissively. "We have a show to do."

Rene couldn't believe her ears. Dumbfounded, she stormed off in search of Mercy.

Senator Stevens, still edging the shadows backstage, approached the table. Parker played it cool. He grabbed a protein bar, leaned up against the wall, and munched.

"I'm not sure this is helping us," the senator said, "and we can't afford to lose those senate votes."

"Cindy went over the line," Parker replied matter-of-factly.

"I know," the senator agreed. "People laugh at an idiot, but they root for an underdog. Sometimes it's a fine line that makes the difference."

"Maybe Cindy is too close to the situation."

"Perhaps."

They stood a few moments in contemplative silence.

"We've got to finish this well," the senator finally continued. "There are millions of dollars on the line."

Parker nodded, taking another swig of his Gatorade. "Just remember—I'm not the one who is neck deep here."

The senator didn't respond. He knew he'd asked a favor and did not want to blow it.

They both turned an eye down the hall toward the stage.

"Guess it's time," Parker noted.

He downed the last swig of his Gatorade, tossed the bottle in the trash, and sauntered back toward the stage. The senator watched him go, an uncharacteristic look of concern painted across his face.

Rachel stepped into Mercy's ready room. Crumpled in a corner, Mercy cried inconsolably. Rachel swooped in and held her crushed daughter tightly in her arms, tears edging her eyes as well.

Rachel was infuriated by Mercy's cruel treatment.

"Let's go home," she said firmly. "They are not gonna treat you like this."

Mercy, unable to speak, nodded in agreement.

At that moment, a contrite Rene stepped into the room. "I'm so sorry about that," Rene offered sympathetically. "I have no idea what is going on."

Rachel, enduring a monumental internal wrestling match, only just managed to hold her rage in check. Even yet, her words poured out with serrated sharpness. "We are going home. I thought you guys did better than this. I guess I was wrong."

"You are right, and you have every right to be upset about this. I am too. But you are our guests. We—*I*—invited you here because I felt that you had something to say, and I would really hate for you to leave before getting a chance to say it."

"They won't even let me talk," Mercy offered.

"She's not going up there again," Rachel asserted.

Rene nodded in understanding. After a moment, however, she hit upon an idea. "What if you went with her?"

Rachel was disinclined to accept the offer. She looked at Mercy questioningly. Mercy returned her gaze.

"Would that be fine?" Rene asked Mercy.

"I did want to talk about Bridget."

"And I want you to," Rene pleaded. "Please?"

Mercy hesitated a few moments, mulling the issue over in her mind. Finally, she screwed up her courage and gave her assent.

Still smoldering, Rachel was reticent. "OK. But any more of this, and we're leaving."

Rene nodded her agreement to this term, and the three women headed back toward the stage.

The tension could be cut with a knife as the ladies stepped out and settled in. The others were already seated, and the audience buzzed somberly. As a national ad played through the monitors, the break clock counted down to what felt like D-day.

The usually calm and gracious Rachel had some choice words for Cindy.

"No one talks to my daughter that way," she seethed under her breath.

An iron coldness in her motherly eyes matched blades with Cindy's steely gaze.

The floor manager began the final countdown as the cue boards lit up.

"Five. Four. Three. Two."

His hand-signal indicated that the show was live, and camera lights flared red. *Parker & Rene* was on the air. Breathless audiences, glued to their screens—many having called friends or relatives to join them, awaited the fallout of this uncharacteristic tongue lashing.

Rene took the lead. "Ladies and Gentlemen, thank you for joining us. I would like to apologize on behalf of our producers for the last segment. We pride ourselves on producing a quality show that is fair minded and respectful. Unfortunately, the last segment was neither. This segment will have a much different tone. Now joining the discussion is Mercy's mother, Rachel Patterson. Rachel is a registered nurse and co-owner of the Patterson Family Clinic with her husband, Dr. Clayton Patterson.

"Rachel, thank you for joining us."

Rachel softened somewhat at hearing Rene's gracious words. The apology was unexpected and genuine. Rachel warmed to Rene.

"It's my pleasure."

"So, Rachel," Rene began.

"I'm sorry, Rene," Cindy interrupted, "can I interject here just a moment?"

Rene opened her mouth to deny that request, when Parker again stepped over her.

"Sure, Cindy," he replied.

"I would like to apologize for my statement as well." Cindy continued, stumbling with uncertainty, "I was . . . a bit . . . harsh. I don't mean disrespect to Mercy. I just feel that the right to Choice is so fundamental to a woman's dignity that I get . . . a little . . . passionate about it."

"That is very understandable," Parker offered.

"I hope there are no hard feelings about my comments."

Rachel and Mercy glanced at each other questioningly. Each distrusted Cindy and were reticent to accept her comments at face value. They made no comment.

Cindy glanced toward the senator. She searched his expression for any sign of approval. She saw none. She saw nothing, in fact. Senator Stevens had mastered his poker face.

The senator glanced at his watch.

The gold face glinted in the light as the senator gauged the time. A diamond highlighted each hour on the Rolex's face, and diamonds rimmed the edge of it. The eighteen-karat gold matched well with the black Georgio Armani tuxedo Senator Stevens wore.

The strains of Bach, Debussy and Wagner wafted through the dance hall as the chamber orchestra stroked their strings. Celebrities and notables of every kind graced the room—semi-pro athletes, minor film stars, local television personalities and notable businesspeople. The senator schmoozed his way through the crowd, champagne in hand. He was the life of the party, bringing laughter to every clique and making each attendee feel as if they were the guest of honor.

The senator's man posted himself in a key spot amid the throng. As the senator passed by, he surreptitiously handed a note to the thug, then waded on into the press. It wasn't long before he ran across Parker and struck up a conversation.

The senator's man took a glance at the note. Hardly a muscle twitched in his countenance as he scanned the scribbles, then slipped it into his pocket. Then, like a palace royal guard, he steadfastly stood his ground.

A new guest arrived. Flashy and a little bombastic, Dr. Morris made his entrance, a knockout escort—barely half his age—in tow. His tuxedo was designed to grab attention like a magnet. The gold satin collar accented the royal-blue wool that composed the bulk of his tailored threads. The jacket was a colonial-cut short jacket with gold rope embroidery and brass buttons, and his two-tone suede wingtips perfectly matched his tux. In keeping with his free-rolling style, he wore the jacket unbuttoned, revealing a gold vest and scarlet scarf tie. His date, a stunning brunette who could easily have been a model, drew gazes of envy with her breathtaking forest-green satin dress. It was a formfitting A-line cut with a simple single shoulder strap. She accented her attire with a dazzling gold choker featuring a scarlet emblem and matching gold earrings.

Greeters stood at the door, taking the guests' coats and guiding them toward the refreshments. Dr. Morris checked in his trench coat, and his date deposited her furs.

A waiter approached, offering wine. The couple took two, then perused brightly through the crowd. They floated, arm in arm, from one conversation to the next. Dr. Morris was self-possessed and confident, and his protégé adroitly hung on his every word.

As they drifted toward the center of the room, the senator's man stepped innocuously from his post and meandered, almost randomly, to encounter the doctor. Upon meeting, he gave the doctor a glance that suggested the girl might want to find another place to be for the moment.

The doctor took the hint. "Darling, why don't you head over and grab us some hors d'oeuvres."

She nodded understandingly and headed back to the wine table. Once she stepped out of earshot, the thug handed over the note. "The senator would like to express his appreciation."

Dr. Morris scanned the note, a curl of a smile flashing across his face as understanding set in. The note read: SB3910 S.1344.a-12.

"Good," the doctor responded, pleased. "He got it included."

"I think you will find the terms acceptable."

As the thug returned to his original post, again taking a circuitous route, the senator glanced toward the doctor, their eyes meeting. With a slight smile, Dr. Morris raised his glass in offer of a silent toast. Senator Stevens lifted his in acknowledgment. The senator turned back to his conversation with Parker just as the doctor's date returned with two small plates of delectable delights.

"Everything OK?" she asked.

"Yes, very well," Dr. Morris replied cheerfully. "Very well indeed."

She smiled warmly, swirled her wine, and took a sip. The refrains of another Debussy number swelled gently through the room. Dr. Morris glanced toward the dance floor, noticing several couples wending their way toward it. With a sweeping gesture, he offered an invitation. "Shall we dance?"

The two sheets lay side by side on the desk. Virtually identical, they shared only one disparity—that they offered starkly different accounts of the same event.

The brightly lit office showcased everything one would expect a doctor to have—except for the grandeur. Shelves of medical journals, anatomies, and journals of pharmacology lined one wall. Reasonably comfortable chairs faced the desk, and medical artifacts of all kinds were scattered tastefully throughout the space. Yet the furniture was functional rather than fabulous, and economy seemed to rule the day.

Dr. Patterson studied the documents that lay before him. Each was an ambulance report from the EMS squad over which he served as medical director. The particulars of the event were the same one page to the next, but the descriptions left him perplexed.

"Why are there conflicting ambulance-run forms?" he asked himself out loud. "Where in the world did *this* come from?!"

Perusing farther through the case folder, he noticed the certificate of death. Leaping from the page were the words "Suicidal Trauma."

"Now wait just a minute!" he exploded. "Suicide!?"

Overhearing his rant, Rachel poked her head in the door. "Are we talking to ourselves again, Doctor?"

"Yes, ma'am. I should listen to myself sometime and see if I make sense."

Rachel chuckled. "You have a patient in room three."

He nodded. Then his jovial tone flew away, replaced by brooding concern. He scanned over the pages again. "I think Janice will want to check into this."

"Why? Do you want to sue someone?" Rachel replied, trying to restore the lightness of the conversation.

"Maybe."

There was a seriousness in his statement that set Rachel aback.

A weight hung in the air as Clayton paused in thought. Then he seemed to shift mental gears. "Room 3, you said?"

"Yes," she replied, "and you do."

"I do?"

"You make sense."

"Well, I can't make sense of this!"

He closed the folder and tossed it to his desk in frustration. He rose from his seat and grabbed his stethoscope as he headed for the door. "Okay, let's see if Mrs. 'Plum' is ripe."

Again, Rachel giggled. Clayton pasted a quick peck on her cheek, and the pair headed down the hall.

It wasn't conspicuous and couldn't have been observed from the doorway, but had she noticed it, this folder would have been particularly important to Rachel. The name on the tab read, *Bridget Matthews*.

CHAPTER SEVEN
Power Shift

Mercy's book lay on the coffee table next to Rene, practically forgotten. Though much more civil, the discussion had grown animated. Rachel and Cindy, both still stinging from their respective sides of the last blowup, were engaged in an intelligent, rapid-fire debate over a landmark Supreme Court case that weighed heavily in the discussion.

"But," Cindy asserted, "the *Roe v. Wade* decision made it very clear that a fetus is *potential* life, *not* an actual person. They said that, given the Constitution's privacy provisions, a woman has a right to do with her own body as she chooses."

"You need to read Section eight of the court's majority decision," Rachel fired back. "The Court ruled that—and I quote—'We, therefore, conclude that the right of personal privacy includes the abortion decision, but that this right is not unqualified, and must be considered against important state interests in regulation.'

"And what about the *Dobbs* Decision? The Justices noted the faulty legal arguments behind *Roe*. They recognized that there is no Constitutional right to an abortion. So, how can you make arguments in favor of abortion based on *Roe*?"

"Now you're an attorney?" Cindy tossed out sarcastically.

"No, but my mother is. Listen, if you can read medical jargon, legalese is a breeze."

The audience tittered a little at her jibe.

"But a fetus isn't a person."

"Have you ever heard of the Dred Scott Decision?"

"No," Cindy replied.

Parker stiffened at the mention of Dred Scott.

"I have heard of it," Parker interjected, "and I don't see—"

Still miffed about how her daughter was treated, Rachel refused to be cut off. She ignored Parker. "You might be interested to know that the Dred Scott decision provided a key precedent for the *Roe v. Wade* decision."

Noticing Cindy's complete lack of familiarity with Dred Scott, Parker tried to turn the discussion. "That's not—"

Rachel reddened and turned to Parker. Her motherly index finger aimed directly at his heart, and her mother's fierceness boiled out. "Parker, you played bully with my daughter. *Do not* run over *me*."

Rachel turned back to Cindy as Parker sat stunned and silent. Calming, Rachel addressed another question to Cindy. "I do not favor the Dred Scott decision, but given our disagreements about this issue, wouldn't you agree it probably was a good ruling?"

Cindy, somewhat bewildered by the dramatic shift in the conversation, decided it was time to bring things back to the matter at hand. "I guess. What's that got to do with anything?"

"I'll get to that. In Section 9 of the *Roe v Wade* majority opinion, the justices argued that, within the legal definition of 'person,' a fetus is not covered and thereby does not enjoy the protections of law—the Fourteenth Amendment, in particular. Would you agree with that?"

"Absolutely!"

"The key argument of the Dred Scott decision was virtually identical."

The ladies locked eyes as Rachel paused to give Cindy a chance to answer. Parker knew where this was going. He opened his mouth to answer, but Cindy didn't notice.

"Then I'd say it was a *great* ruling. Advancing the cause of women is always a great thing."

"The Dred Scott case," Parker interjected, "was *not* a case advancing the cause of women. It dealt with the issue of civil rights!"

"Exactly!" Rachel fired back. "The court ruled in *Dred Scott v. Sanford* that a Negro was not a person, or 'citizen,' as the court referred to it, and thereby did not enjoy rights under the law."

"Which is utterly outrageous," Parker added angrily.

Rachel nodded. "In the words of then Chief Justice Taney, blacks 'had no rights which the white man was bound to respect.'"

"What?" Cindy exclaimed, "That has nothing to do with—"

"That is *exactly* the same argument you are using. A fetus should not enjoy the protection of law because it is not a person. *You* are siding with the pro-slavery crowd when you use the same arguments they use to defend the same kind of injustice they were defending."

Cindy, realizing she had stepped into a trap, backpedaled frantically.

"That's not true! I never—"

"In fact," Rachel asserted, "the abortion industry *continues* to side with those who subjugate African Americans."

Parker couldn't contain himself. "Now hold on!"

"By percentage, how much of America is African American?" Rachel questioned.

Neither Parker nor Cindy offered an answer. Whether they knew or not wasn't clear to the audience. The question hung in the air momentarily, then, with deep satisfaction, Rene broke into the conversation that seemed frozen in time.

"About 12 percent," she said exultantly.

"Right," Rachel responded.

Parker, reanimated by his realization that Cindy's arguments were about to get trounced, stepped in. "I see what you're—"

Again, Rachel stopped him with a commanding gesture—just as a schoolteacher might. She continued her train of thought. "Yet African American women represent more than one-third of *all* abortions performed. Abortion, according to the CDC, is the *leading* cause of death among African Americans. And where are clinics routinely located?"

"At airports. Where else?" Cindy shot back sarcastically. She folded her arms in subconscious denial of the statement.

"Two recent studies," Rachel continued, "demonstrated that Planned Parenthood routinely located their clinics in densely populated *minority* neighborhoods. So where is yours?"

Cindy froze, her mouth half open in a response that wouldn't come. Her mind fluttered with indecision over what to say. She'd failed to notice the trap, and now everything she was saying seemed to get twisted into some massive malevolent plot.

She couldn't sidestep or deny Rachel's claim, or she would appear weak. But though she was proud of the service her clinic provided to African Americans in her area, she couldn't acknowledge it, or she would appear evil. And she didn't know enough about Rachel to zing her back with some tidbit of her past and put her on the run. In fact, she'd tried already, but Rachel simply parried the jab deftly and finished with a thrust of her own. All the standard responses failed, and Cindy had momentarily lost trust in her ability to think on her feet and anticipate the outcome. With the bill in the balance and the senator looking on, a wrong move here might be disastrous.

"I would certainly like to know the answer to that question," Rene offered, iciness chilling her words.

Cindy finally found her voice. "But African Americans are people, and they *do* enjoy the rights we all share. Fetuses are not."

Mercy jumped into the fray. "Why aren't they? What changes?"

"They have been born, of course," Cindy shot back, with a "duh" in her tone.

"So," Rachel retorted, "an eight-inch change in *location* determines whether someone can be protected by the law or not?"

Again, the conversation was going the wrong way in Cindy's mind. The stock answers she'd delivered in numerous other encounters simply brought out more questions she couldn't— or wouldn't—answer. She scrambled desperately to bring the conversation back on track with her key talking points.

"You are all clouding the issue. Though the Supreme Court passed the matter to the states, the right to Choice is still a fundamental constitutional right."

"It seems, Cindy," Rene shot back, "that *you* are avoiding the question."

"How can you call it choice," Mercy questioned, emotion choking her words, "when you don't give women enough information to *make* a real choice?"

Cindy forced a smile and took on what she believed to be a motherly tone. "Mercy, darling—"

"Don't patronize my daughter," Rachel retorted.

"Look, I don't mean to be disrespectful," Cindy fired back, "but you don't know what goes on in our clinics. You only know what the anti-choice extremists have told you."

"My friend was hardly an anti-choice extremist. She—"

As Mercy began to head toward the topic of her friend, Parker perked up. Mercy had made some claims about clinics, so he steered the conversation back to Cindy for her expert take on the clinic experience.

"Cindy, for our audiences' benefit, could you, perhaps, describe what *actually* goes on at your clinics?"

Rene's narrowed eyes shot daggers at Parker. She got the intense impression that he was more invested in a specific outcome of the discussion than to respectfully present all sides as he typically did.

"Certainly, Parker." Cindy replied, secretly grateful to have the pressure pulled off her shoulders. "It is very important to us that all of our clients get accurate up-to-date information about their pregnancy and their rights. Each woman is privately counseled by our knowledgeable, compassionate staff."

The ink pen wasn't fancy. It didn't sparkle or even have any real stand-out features. It was a cheap plastic Bic, and the only color on it was the words printed in bright-orange ink—"New Dawn Women's Clinic." But it was there, right on the table, within her to reach. Needing a place to exert her nervous energy, she mindlessly fidgeted with the pen, clicking it and tapping it on the table.

Bridget sat tensely, trying to make sense of her strange environment as she waited for the counselor to arrive. This was the last place in the world she'd expected to be. Though her chair was comfortable, she couldn't relax, and her shoulders were sore from the stress. She took in every detail of the space but did not comprehend it all.

The counseling room was quiet and sober—nothing flashy or inordinate. The walls were a sort of moon gray. Practical. Easy to clean. Easy to decorate. And cheap. A single fluorescent light fixture cast a contrasty green pall over the posters, which featured happy young women touting messages like, "YOUR BODY, YOUR CHOICE."

The table at which Bridget sat centered the space. Three chairs were arranged around it—two on her side and one on the other. A single medical model of a women's reproductive system rested before her on the table, and a few colorful flyers lay neatly nearby. One flyer featured the bold title, "I made the RIGHT choice." She picked it up and perused the bright testimonials from liberated young women who were proud to have chosen abortion.

After some minutes, a pleasantly plump nurse with strawberry-blond hair stepped into the room. Dressed in a white lab coat and wearing a blue stethoscope around her neck, she looked official and authoritative.

This was Nurse Kelly. Bridget looked at her with nervous expectancy. Kelly slid a folder onto the table and sat opposite her. There was a pregnant pause before the nurse delivered her news.

"The test came back positive," Kelly declared with sober compassion. "You are about fifteen or sixteen weeks along, OK? The fee for that here is 1,075 dollars."

Bridget was shaken. She'd hoped against hope that she would never hear those words, but now that they'd spilled out into the cold air, the whole situation seemed too surreal. "Are you sure?"

Kelly looked at Bridget with an expression of deep concern. "Have you missed a period?"

"A couple of them," Bridget responded shakily.

"The test is positive. Do you want to continue this pregnancy?"

"I . . . I don't think so."

The nurse pulled out a form, slid it onto the table, and began to fill it out. She asked Bridget some questions, to which rather uncertain answers were given.

"How old are you?"

"Fourteen." Bridget nervously added, "Um, they don't want to know, like, who is . . . who the father is, do they?"

Nurse Kelly paused, pen poised over the paper, and leaned forward on her elbows. "Will that be a problem?"

"Well," Bridget responded, struggling for words, "I, like, met him at a party."

"So, you don't know who he is?"

"I do . . ."

"Whatever you say to us in these walls cannot be shared with anyone—even your parents."

"If I tell, I would, like, get in a lot of trouble—"

"OK. I understand."

"'Cause, I mean, he's, like, twenty, and . . . well—"

Kelly sighed loudly, interrupting Bridget, and shook her head. "Let's refocus on the details we need here."

A little surprised, Bridget continued, "But couldn't he get in trouble?"

"I don't want to know how old he is, OK?"

"What do you mean?"

"I don't *want* to know how old he is. OK?" the nurse emphasized.

Kelly paused to allow the import of her words to sink in. Bridget still didn't seem to understand the issue at hand, so Kelly continued to explain. "Because in this state," she offered in hushed tones, "anyone fourteen years and younger, um, there has to be, um, a report done to CPS, you know."

"But I'm afraid—"

Bridget couldn't speak her fears. The thought of what the man might do, how her parents would respond, how her church friends and classmates would reproach her, was overwhelming. As her worries compounded, more thoughts flew, more fears grew, and her tension heightened. Nurse Kelly let her stew in her thoughts for a few long moments.

"Well, we deal with this sort of thing all the time. There's really nothing to be afraid of."

Kelly's reassurance loosened Bridget's tongue, but didn't relieve her tension, so she rambled. "You know, 'cause I wasn't supposed to be there."

"Just so you know, in this state, if any adult has had intercourse with a child fourteen or younger, it has to be reported to Child Protective Services. It could be reported as rape, which would be child abuse."

Bridget paled and began to shake, moisture springing to her eyes.

"OK. Listen," Kelly offered, trying to calm her. "I didn't hear the age because, you know, as long as it was consensual—"

Bridget looked as if she might be sick and began to cry. She drew her knees up under her chin, hooking her heels on the edge of the seat, and hugged her legs.

Nurse Kelly realized that it might have been a rape situation, so she shifted gears. "Look, you don't have to be afraid of the father. We can just take care of this, and it's all over. You never have to think about it again. You don't really want a daily reminder of what happened, do you?"

Bridget shook her head.

"So, for the father, you could just say—" Kelly paused to let Bridget gather her thoughts and to think through her story.

Bridget dried her eyes. She struck upon a promising thought and pitched it tentatively. "So, if I say, like, I don't really know who the father was, but he's, like, one of the guys at school or something?"

"Right." Kelly nodded. "You know, you've seen him around, whatever. You know he's fourteen, he's in your grade, and . . . you know."

Bridget nodded in agreement.

"You just put this whole thing behind you," Kelly said consolingly. "Now, you should know that in this state, you would need to get a form signed by your parents in order to get a procedure here."

"You're not going to tell my parents, are you?" Bridget worried.

"We can't say anything to your parents. Federal HIPAA law forbids us to tell anyone, OK? But somehow, we must have a form like that in our files in order to do a procedure."

Bridget nodded.

"Look. Here's what I can do for you, OK?" She flipped through the folder and pulled out a paper with the names, addresses, and contact information for six other abortion clinics.

"Now, I'm going to *give* you this because I cannot *tell* you this, OK? But I can show you."

"OK." Bridget moved closer to get a good view of the sheet.

The nurse circled an address, then tapped it for emphasis with the clicker side of her pen so it wouldn't leave a mark.

Bridget leaned in and took a good look. "So, this one is, like, outside the state?"

Kelly nodded, mentally reminding herself not to actually speak.

"But now I'm going to do this so that—you know—"

Kelly circled all the clinics and gave Bridget the sheet. Bridget folded it and stuck it in her purse. She glanced back up and caught sight of the female reproductive model.

Nurse Kelly had begun to jot notes so was not expecting the next question.

"Is it a baby now?"

"No, no," Kelly responded, almost absentmindedly. "It's developing, but there is no brain activity. It is just fetal tissue."

"So, it's not a baby?"

Kelly looked up from the form and met Bridget's eyes. "It's not a living, breathing baby at this point, if that's what you mean, and if you were to deliver it right now, it would not live."

Kelly paused, waiting for Bridget to cast out another question.

Instead, Bridget simply nodded in assent. Then she had another realization. "I can't go to another state. My parents will find out for sure."

Kelly leaned forward, hands folded under her chin thoughtfully.

"Hmmm." She thought for a few moments, then had an idea. "Excuse me for a moment."

She rose and stepped from the room. After a few moments, she returned, Cindy in tow.

Cindy was dressed in a charcoal gray power suit with a collared white blouse and a small red scarf that served as a feminine version of a necktie. Her heels clicked sharply with every step, and her warm—almost patronizing—smile communicated to Bridget that she was a friend.

"This is Cindy, our administrator," Kelly introduced, "and she can help us, sometimes, with, you know, special cases like yours."

Bridget nodded.

Cindy slipped into the seat next to Bridget and expressed her sympathy. "Nurse Kelly has explained your situation to me. I want you to know, I really sympathize with your situation. I will do all I can to help you. Do you have an older sibling, over eighteen, who could sign? You know, as long as you share the same last name—"

Cindy faded off, and Bridget caught the implication. She shook her head.

"No, I am an only child. And I don't know how I can get the money."

"You know," Cindy suggested sweetly, "we can help you get money for the procedure from the father. He should expect to have consequences from his decisions."

"But I'm afraid he—"

Bridget paused, her unspoken fears ringing loudly in the room.

"Isn't there, like, some kind of free—like, a grant or something?" she asked finally.

"Well, there is in some rare circumstances. We don't yet get public funds in this state. A few groups do provide funding in certain circumstances, but unfortunately, because of your age, we would not be able to get you approved for any of them."

Bridge's concern mounted, and the worry was evident in her face. Abandoning her sweet tone, Cindy became firmer and more direct, though not, by any means, offensive.

"Listen, if you are concerned about contacting the father, we could set you up with a payment plan, but you should know that you must have the account paid in full before the procedure, and for each week you wait, the procedure grows more costly. It's really in your best interests to take care of this as soon as possible."

Bridget cried quietly again. She felt trapped with no way out. The shame of how others would respond, the despair for having made mistakes that led to this moment—all crashed in on her, and she felt powerless to find a way through.

"When you can come up with the money, we will find a way to help you, all right?"

Cindy rose, stepped to the door, and with a motion, indicated that the counseling session was over. Bridget glumly rose, alone and ashamed. The tears, though assuaged, continued to trickle from her dark eyes.

As she passed through, an aide handed a note to Cindy, who unfolded it and saw it was from Senator Stevens. She looked up as the aide commented, eyes rolling.

"He's on our case about quotas again."

Irritated, Cindy shot back, "Unless he plans to offer procedures for free, he should be happy that we get what we get!"

CHAPTER EIGHT

Brat

Rachel sat on the edge of her seat, offering a passionate response to Cindy. There was a bit of heat in her cheeks as she spoke. "Abortion clinics don't offer freedom of choice. They only give one option—pay the money and get rid of the baby."

"That's not true," Cindy fired back. "We give *all* the options to our patients—"

"What about adoption?" Rachel interjected, "How many adoption referrals have you had in the last year?"

Uncomfortable with the question, Cindy went on autopilot, falling back on the canned answers she'd rehearsed countless times for just such occasions as these. "How can you ask that?! Adoption is far too traumatizing to women. Imagine carrying an infant for nine months, then just handing it off to total strangers."

"What about open adoptions? That way a mother can be an active part of her child's life without the burden of raising a child she can't support. Do you ever suggest that as an option?"

"Can you just see how a mother's heart is torn out every time she has to say goodbye to her child? How cruel do you have to be to put her through that?"

Rachel was stunned by the selfishness of Cindy's assertions. Every argument was solely about the mother and how she felt without regard to anyone else—the infant, the father, the grandparents. The utter narcissistic self-possession of every response lit Rachel up. Her face burned red, tears sprung to her eyes, and her mother's fiery passion scorched through her every word.

"Then what about all of the birthdays, and the first steps, and the Christmases, and the first dates, and the graduations—*everything* a mother misses when her child is *dead*. How much does *that* tear a mother's heart out? And what about the child? Don't you think the child would want to live if you ever asked her?"

A deep agony in Cindy's own soul rose to meet Rachel's passion. Her eyes lit up, and a long-repressed but razor-sharp guilt gave an edge to her reply. "What if she was abused or neglected? How do you think she would feel about her mother's selfish little choice then?"

"So," Rachel retorted, "burning a child to death in salt, or tearing her limb from limb, or ripping her from her mother's womb and stabbing her in the back of the neck is *not* child abuse? What planet are you from?"

"What do you know?" Cindy screamed. "Have you ever been in this situation? What right do you have to tell me that I don't have the right to choose? I help women make the *right* choice—the choice *not* to be burdened with a stinking little brat that will ruin their lives!"

Rachel was taken aback. The entire studio was stunned by Cindy's seemingly heartless exclamation.

Rachel's wet eyes became a waterway. The emotion that tore from her heart choked her words so she could hardly speak, yet the power of her response rang like gongs throughout the studio. "A child isn't a brat. She is a treasure!!"

Looking over her director's shoulder, Catherine instinctively knew what the next shot should be.

"Cut to Mercy," Catherine shouted. "Go on Camera Three!"

With a quick pan and the punch of a button, her orders were carried out.

Looming large in the frame was Mercy. Her tearful half smile of pride and gratefulness was the most eloquent thing she'd said all day. Every viewer could see just how much she loved and appreciated her mother. Her gloved hand rose to wipe away a tear, then she reached over, clasped hands with her mother, and squeezed. The two locked eyes, sharing an instant "I love you" as they often had over the years.

Mercy knew she could always count on her mother's love.

A little fog gathered on the glass as a very young nose pressed against the pane. Two eager eyes peered through, searching the clinic lobby for just one person—her mother.

Janice pulled the handle on the door—gently, so she wouldn't hurt little Mercy's nose. The pair entered, announced by a tinkling bell hanging from the door. Megan, the cheerful, people-loving receptionist, looked up, and a broad toothy smile spread across her face. Megan was something like a young Queen Latifa with a day job—boundless energy and endless heart.

"Look busy, everyone," Megan exclaimed. "Our head nurse is here. How are you, Mercy, honey!"

Five-year-old Mercy was dressed in a cute mini-nurse outfit. Proud of her mother, she loved dressing up and "helping" Rachel at the clinic. She bounded over to the counter to greet Megan and was offered an affectionate hug.

Mercy wrapped her arms around Megan's neck, but her left arm was rather stiff, and she couldn't give a tight squeeze. Megan barely noticed. She was used to Mercy hugs. Mercy carried a wicked-looking scar that ran virtually the full length of her left arm—from the end of her stiff and deformed pinkie finger to her shoulder. It was an old wound with deep twists, peaks, and ravines. It wound tightly in some places, making it difficult for Mercy to move the arm. While children, in their innocence, would often ask about it—or maybe even tease—the adults at the clinic made no issue whatsoever about Mercy's injury.

Janice stepped to the counter behind her. "Megan, please tell me you're not too busy. I've got to file for a court order today! Is it OK to drop Mercy off a smidge early?"

"We're a little behind, but it should be all right. Let me page Rachel."

Just then Rachel appeared in the lobby to call her next patient, but she brightened when she saw Mercy.

"Hi, honey! Did you have a good time with Grammy?"

"I'm a nurse, Mommy!"

"So I see!"

"I'm sorry, Rachel," Janice interjected, "but I got a call that could change the case I'm working on. Could I leave Mercy with you?"

"Let me clear this with Dr. Patterson. Megan, can you help?"

"Sure! I'll just put her to work." Megan winked at Mercy.

"Mommy, who is Dr. Patterson?"

"Clay is Dr. Patterson," Rachel whispered.

"Clay?" Mercy asked incredulously.

Dr. Patterson—Clay—popped into the lobby, patient in tow, to schedule a new appointment. Always pleasant and cheerful, the good doctor was bantering with the mother-to-be when he caught sight of Mercy. He smiled brightly, and Mercy ran excitedly into his arms.

"Clay!"

"Well, hi there, Mercy!" Clayton responded. "How's my favorite little nurse today?"

Rachel colored a bit. She was embarrassed that her familiar references to Dr. Patterson at home had piqued Mercy's ears and made it back to him. She hoped he didn't put it all together.

"Mercy, we call him Dr. Patterson here!"

"But, Mommy, at home you said—"

"Mercy, please! This is Dr. Patterson's clinic."

Megan and Janice shared a knowing look, then Megan turned to help her patient pick a day for the next go-around. Rachel became flustered. She was certain her secret would be exposed—and in public, right in the lobby of the clinic. She couldn't imagine a more embarrassing moment. Clayton, however, seemed oblivious to Rachel's consternation and the others' glances.

"Do you want to grow up to help people like Mommy does?" he asked the diminutive nurse.

"Uh-huh."

Needing to get his permission for Mercy to stay—and with the secret hope of shifting the subject—Rachel interjected, "I'm sorry, Doctor. Would it be all right for Mercy to stay here? My mother needs to meet someone right away. Megan will help me watch her."

"If Megan agrees."

Megan had just finished with the appointment and glanced over, smiling.

"Oh sure. It won't be any trouble. Mercy is a doll."

Mercy played with Clayton's stethoscope. "What's this?"

"That's my stethoscope, sweetheart," the doctor replied.

"Grammy said you keep it in the fridge."

Clayton laughed lightly. "She did, did she?" His eyes twinkled mischievously. "For *her* I will!"

Janice merely laughed in response and turned to Rachel.

"I need to go."

She bid everyone farewell. Dr. Patterson set Mercy down, gave her a wink, and headed back to his office. Megan handed Rachel a clipboard for the next patient, and Rachel perused the chart. She locked eyes with the patient and invited her back to the waiting room.

Megan grabbed a toy doctor's bag and invited Mercy to join her behind the counter.

"Here, honey. You can be a nurse right here where I can help you."

"Thank you, Miss Megan."

"You're welcome, honey."

Mercy began to play, time ticking away unnoticed.

Patients came and went. The lobby hung in anticipatory quietness, occasionally punctuated by momentary conversation. Before anyone had realized, three hours ticked off. The sun settled low on the horizon, long shadows filling the lobby as Mercy busied herself cleaning up toys. The clock ticked past 7:00 p.m. and kept on going. The clinic was empty of all but staff—and one adorable little girl. From the back-nurse's station, Rachel hauled a stack of forms and charts that needed to be entered and filed.

"Whew! Megan, I owe you a pedicure! Thanks for watching Mercy!"

"She's so sweet, Rachel, it was no problem at all."

"We are so late! You go, and I'll shut things down for the night."

Megan practically dropped everything in her hands right on the reception desk and kicked into high gear. She had places to be, and with the lateness of their parting, very little time to get there.

"You don't have to ask me twice," she replied, laughing.

Rachel chuckled as Megan went into turbo mode, grabbed her handbag and keys, and darted out the exit.

But before closing the door, Megan turned back and bid her farewell. "Thanks, Rach! See you tomorrow."

"Good night."

"Good night, honey," Megan affectionately offered Mercy.

"Good night, Miss Megan."

Megan closed the door, then dashed to her nearby car.

Clayton slipped into the lobby, leafing through a client chart. He closed the file and noticed that Rachel and Mercy were still there.

"What a day! I've sure earned my overtime!" he said.

"I'm exhausted," Rachel replied.

"Hey, Rachel, Janice is going to be late, and it has been a long day. Why don't I treat you ladies to dinner?"

"That just might save my life. Thank you."

Rachel glanced over to Mercy and noticed that she had gotten distracted by a particularly interesting toy. "Mercy, hurry and pick things up. We're going to eat out.

"Oh, goody! Can I have pancakes?"

Clayton and Rachel laughed at Mercy's remark. Clayton headed for the coat closet. "Let me get our coats and we'll be on our way."

A low murmur carried through the intimately darkened dining room. Little clinks and tinks rang out as the various guests enjoyed their feasts. Busy waiters in shirts and bow ties offered punctual service, taking orders, delivering dishes, and filling cups with near military precision.

Each table featured a centerpiece with three electric candles flickering with a warm glow. Some tables were square and others round. Some promised cozy booth seating, while others sported plush chairs. Clayton, Rachel, and Mercy sat at a small square table. Each chair had an armrest, which, at the moment, Mercy was using as an imaginary horse for her doll to ride. Drinks, place settings, and menus sat before them, and except for occasional sips, were generally ignored as Rachel and Clayton chatted.

"I don't really like to talk about it," Rachel commented, answering one of Clayton's questions. "It makes me sound like a whiner."

"I asked," Clayton replied encouragingly, "because I really want to know how a single mom can have a professional life. You do it so easily."

"Easily!" Rachel exclaimed with a laugh. "Today was a train wreck. If you only knew! Mom helps a lot, but she has her own firm, and . . . to do childcare? It's hard."

"But you seem to have it all together."

"There are times I just feel like crying myself to sleep. I barely feel presentable when I get to work every day."

"What do you mean? You're beautiful."

A slight smile traced across his face, and his eyes sparkled a bit.

Rachel was embarrassed by the complement. "Thanks," she replied, blushing, "but sometimes, I just don't know what to do. I feel like a failure as a mother."

"I'm sorry that you feel that way, Rachel, because you are a great mother."

"Dr. Patterson," Rachel replied soberly, "Mercy is a wonderful girl, but I know she needs more than I can give her myself."

Clayton took a businesslike tone. "Rachel, how long have you worked for me?"

Rachel thought for a moment. "Mercy is five, so almost that long—why?"

"For people who work together that long, a first-name basis is still professional, isn't it?"

Rachel looked into his eyes, surprised by what she heard that he *didn't* say. The glow in her cheeks deepened, and she glanced away. The conversation was growing awkward, when it was blissfully interrupted by the waitress.

"May I take your order please?"

Clayton was a bit startled but quickly recovered. "Oh. I'll have the shrimp fettuccini with Caesar salad please."

"I'd like the chicken parmesan with garden salad and Italian dressing on the side," Rachel added. "And the chocolate smile pancake for Mercy. With milk, please."

The waitress glanced at Mercy as she jotted down the order. Sparkling little eyes framed by a little nurse's bonnet smiled up at her. The waitress smiled back. "So, the little nurse gets the happy pancakes!" she exclaimed. "Sir, your daughter is just about the cutest thing I've ever seen!"

"She's not my daughter," Clayton replied, "but I wouldn't mind if she were."

Rachel blushed as their eyes met again. Slowly a warm smile grew on her face.

The diminutive nurse was completely sacked out. It had been a long day for her five short years. Rachel juggled her daughter, her purse, and the doorknob as she entered her home.

Porch light spilled through the open door, painting a streak of brilliance across the floor. The lights were low, giving a warm—almost romantic—glow to the kitchen. Janice, enjoying a quiet moment to snack and read, sat at the table. As the pair entered, she rose to help. Rachel pressed the door shut with her heel and plopped her purse on the table.

"Oh, the poor dear," Janice whispered. "Long day?"

Rachel vibrated inside from the remarkable evening, her cheeks still carrying a bit of rosiness that belied her repressed excitement.

"Mother, we need to talk."

"Uh, sure," Janice replied, "Here, lay her on the bed."

Janice bent over the nearby daybed and arranged the pillows and throw to make a comfortable space for the slumbering child. Rachel laid Mercy down gently and tucked the throw around her, careful not to wake her. She stood, gazing at her daughter with motherly pride.

"What's going on?" Janice asked, concerned.

Rachel moved back to the table, taking a seat across from her mother's coffee cup and breadcrumbs.

"Mom, I can hardly believe a day can change so much. Clay treated Mercy and me to dinner."

"Okay," Janice commented, hardly able to contain her excitement.

"And he asked me if I thought it would be unprofessional if a doctor dated a nurse employee."

A delighted sparkle flashed across Janice's eyes. "Really! What did you say?"

"I almost told him what I was thinking but managed to at least act clinical about it."

"So, what *did* you say?"

"If they are honest and discreet so it would not affect patient care, it should be OK."

"So, what did you *want* to say?"

"If you're talking about me, it's about time!"

They shared a quiet giggle.

"I always thought he'd be good for you," Janice offered.

"Now, Mom, we just agreed to date! Don't get ahead of me!"

"I think it'd be hard to catch up with you!" Janice teased.

"Mom!"

"What about Mercy?"

"That's just it! He really loves her! He is so gentle with her. She is positively in awe of Clay."

"Like you?"

Rachel blushed again and glanced down, fiddling absentmindedly with her gold bracelet. "Yeah, I guess. Mom, Clay is the first man I can ever say that I totally trust."

Janice took a sip of her coffee, holding the cup poised in her hands to allow the warmth to trickle into her fingers. "That's how love grows," Janice offered thoughtfully. "It shows how important our every decision can be."

"What do you mean?"

"You chose life."

Rachel nodded. A small smile crawled across her face, and her heart glowed with hope. She'd often wondered whether she'd made the right choice. But with life comes love, and every dream she held dear was becoming embodied in this precious little girl with a heart as big as all outdoors.

CHAPTER NINE

Tragedy

The applause died back as Rene turned to face the camera.

"We are back," Rene began. "For those of you who just joined us, we have with us Mercy Patterson, a young lady who, at the age of fourteen, wrote a book entitled *An Angel's Blood.* She is here to discuss her views, as expressed in the book, on women's reproductive rights."

"Also, with us is Cindy Pierce," Parker added, nearly cutting her off, "administrative director of the New Dawn Women's Clinics."

Parker immediately turned to Cindy and lobbed a leading, softball question. "Cindy, the anti-abortion protestors have often accused clinics such as New Dawn of using dangerous procedures. Could you describe the policies you have in place to protect against these concerns?"

With her practiced positive, cheerful demeanor, Cindy glibly answered his question. "Of course, Parker. The facilities are inspected regularly, just like hospitals are. The conditions are germ-free and sterile. Every precaution is taken to protect the health of the mother. Each patient is closely monitored for as long as she needs. When she is released, each patient is in excellent condition and can be certain that she is ready to return to her desired life."

"That sounds pretty good to me," Parker stated, looking directly at Mercy. "What problem do you have with that?"

"It doesn't really work that way," Mercy countered.

"Are you saying that there are no inspections, that the facilities are filthy, that there's no recovery room or care? Come on."

"I didn't say that! But it isn't safe like she says."

"Ms. Patterson," Parker queried incredulously, "have you ever been inside a clinic?"

"Yes, I have."

Parker's mind froze mid-thought. In the past, everyone he'd asked that of had said no. He would then dismantle them like a first-year biology student dicing a dead frog. Never had he encountered someone who'd said yes who wasn't already on his side. His normal MO was out the window, and he was uncertain of what to do next. Given the fiasco earlier, he couldn't just call her a liar or dismiss her outright. It would merely pique the audience interest, and they would demand detail. He couldn't just let it slide. He'd lose credibility.

And then there was the possibility she was *there* that day.

Cindy was also taken aback. It suddenly struck her that she had underestimated Mercy. Dismissing her as a Right-wing nut, she hadn't even bothered to page through the book. Now, she'd been hit with a bombshell. She thought that Mercy could either be a hypocrite or a repentant mother but couldn't tell which. Being unfamiliar with Mercy's story—and with so much egg on her face already—she couldn't be the first to accuse or question the teen in that way.

As Cindy combed her mind for an appropriate way to respond, Mercy continued.

"Some women *die* from abortions."

Parker and Cindy grew nervous. The conversation was, again, veering dangerously close to the topic they both wanted desperately to stay away from. *Miles* away.

"That does *not* happen," Cindy asserted vehemently. "It has *never* happened under my watch."

"Really?" Mercy exclaimed. "Cindy, do you ever answer the phone at your clinic?"

Cindy opened her mouth to cast out another terse zinger, but she couldn't. Nothing came out. She had no idea what to answer. Cindy paled and, after a moment, she managed to croak out a strange response.

"What? *You*?"

Realization hit like a ton of bricks. She suddenly understood that Mercy had been on the other end of the line that night. She could say no more.

Rene, reading the moment, took that chance to play her ace. "Mercy, who was Bridget Matthews?"

"Bridget was my best friend," Mercy replied, emotion threatening to drown her words. "We did just about everything together."

Parker, Cindy, and Senator Stevens all shared a glance. Despite their best efforts, the situation was clear. The jig was up. Mercy would talk, and the progress that had been made on the funding bill would evaporate.

Mercy fiddled absentmindedly with her "Choose Life" bracelet.

A can clattered as it shot down the gray concrete walkway. It had been propelled with a swift kick by a sneaker-clad foot. Two chatting teen girls, obviously close friends, sauntered down the walk. Their neighborhood was a quiet, upscale middle-class cul-de-sac. The sounds of kids running in their back yards or a teen shooting hoops echoed faintly across the way. An occasional Lexus, Mercedes, or Suburban whispered by, but the community remained chill.

Mercy and Bridget were lost in conversation as they walked home from school. Mercy wore her backpack over her shoulder, while Bridget swung hers in a graceful arc with every step. They each looked like your average teen, dressed in T-shirts, jeans, and sneakers, except for Mercy's ever-present long black glove and red "Choose Life" bracelet.

Both girls were pushing fifteen and had become fast friends when Bridget's family moved into the neighborhood years ago. Attending the same church, going to the same school, and running with the same friends kept them in nearly constant contact with each other. They discussed everything and shared secrets even sisters didn't get to know. And like most teens, the conversation often turned to boys.

"Mercy, Jason is, like, a really nice guy. He just thinks you're, like, a little stuck-up."

"Why?" Mercy wondered.

"The glove."

"*He'd* be a little stuck-up if he knew what was under it."

"I don't think so. He's not that way—and he's, like, really into you."

Mercy looked at her friend accusingly, panicking a bit. "You didn't tell—"

"Are you crazy? Best friends never tell. Your secret is safe with me."

They bumped shoulders in solidarity and giggled, as close friends do.

Mercy changed the subject. "Are you guys ready for the district finals tomorrow?"

"I think so, but, like, I probably won't go," Bridget replied.

"What! Why not?" Mercy was shocked. Bridget was, perhaps, the best volleyball player on the JV team. Her serve was deadly and very well could take them to state for the first time in eight years.

Bridget got very quiet and thoughtful.

"Bridget, what's wrong?"

Bridget walked on a few more paces, a fiery battle waging within her. "Best friends never tell, right?"

"Bridget, what—"

"Promise me, Mercy," Bridget urged.

Mercy paused undecidedly. She'd always been taught to be truthful and keep her promises, but she'd also been cautioned to only promise wisely. She hesitated.

"Please!"

"OK," Mercy promised uncertainly.

"Alice and I went to that party at Bryson's house."

"What!? Bridget, he's in college!"

"I know," Bridget replied, "but, like, we heard all of the other girls talking about it, and, like, they made it sound fire."

"So, what happened?"

"Well"—Bridget struggled for words—"we, like, dressed up and got a couple IDs from her sister, just in case. But they let us in and didn't check anything. And, like, all kinds of things were going on—music, dancing. Guys were handing out beers."

"So, you got drunk?"

"Yeah, a little. All those hot college guys were talking to us and giving us, like, stuff."

"How did you get home?"

"Well . . . that's not really, like, all that happened."

"Bridget!"

"I got feeling, like, a little sick, so, like, Bryson walked me up to a bedroom upstairs to lay down and everything. I kind of passed out, I think, but when I came to, he was on top of me. He—"

"Oh no."

Bridget choked up, and tears sprung to her eyes.

Mercy patted her shoulder compassionately.

"I didn't know what to do. I just, like, I let him."

"What . . . what happened then?"

"When he was done, he just, like, got up and left. I was so sick, I crawled to the bathroom and, like, threw up."

"Oh, Bridget," Mercy offered, crying softly, "what did your parents say?"

"I never told them. I . . . I told them I was, like, going to your house!"

"Bridget, you need to tell them."

"That's not the worst of it." Bridget grew even more serious.

Mercy trembled at the thought of what Bridget might have to say.

"Mercy, I'm pregnant."

"Bridget, no! Are you sure?"

"My mom and dad will *kill* me if they find out!! You have to promise that you won't tell them!"

"But, Bridget, you can't hide it for long."

Bridget looked to the sidewalk, fighting back shame and embarrassment.

"There's one way. There's this clinic. I, like, talked to someone there."

Bridget glanced up to Mercy to gauge her response and immediately saw Mercy's dismay.

"Mercy, this thing could ruin my whole life! I wouldn't get to go to college or have a career. I'll be trapped, and, like, Mom and Dad would never understand! This way it is all taken care of, and my parents never have to know!"

"But how can you kill your baby? Bridget, you *know* that's wrong!"

Panic rose in Bridget's throat, and her cheeks flushed.

"But I can't, like, face Mom and Dad! I can't face the kids at school or church."

"C'mon, Bridget. You know you will have to sometime. It will be hard, but most everyone will forgive you. You know I will!"

"No!" Bridget shook her head vehemently. "No one can find out! I have to undo this somehow."

"But, Bridget, the truth always comes out. God already knows!"

"Well, why did He let this happen to me!?"

"I don't know, but God will forgive you if you just ask."

Bridget grew defensive. "Mercy, you don't know what it's like! Besides, it's not my fault! It's not like I asked to get—"

Bridget couldn't quite get the word out. She practically gagged on it. She began to shake, much as she did at the clinic, and the tears flowed freely.

"I know you didn't, but it did happen. Just—*please*, don't do this."

"You have never gone through anything like this! Why should one mistake ruin the rest of my life?!"

"Oh, Bridget! At least promise me you'll talk to my mom before you do anything else, please."

"I'll think about it. Just don't tell anybody, OK?"

Mercy reluctantly nodded her head.

The pair walked on silently for a couple more houses until they arrived at Bridget's doorstep.

The girls faced each other for a long moment, then Bridget squeezed Mercy's hand as a gesture of thanks, mounted the stairs, and opened the door. She turned to Mercy, gave a little wave, and stepped inside.

Mercy stood for a few uncertain moments, pondering the bombshell her dearest friend had just dropped on her.

With a deep sigh, she turned and walked on.

The water splashed as the scrubber passed over a grimy plate.

Mercy stood over the kitchen sink, washing off the remnants of a delectable family dinner. A long yellow dish glove had replaced her standard black lace glove. Her flowery apron was already spotted with splashes of soapy dishwater.

Her iPhone lit up, playing the familiar 'frains of Michael W. Smith's "I Will Be Your Friend"—Mercy's ringtone for Bridget. Anxious, Mercy ripped off her dish glove and answered the phone. "Hey, Bridget."

Mercy listened for a moment, then panic streaked across her face.

"What! Where are you!? … I'll be right there!" Mercy dashed for the door.

"Mercy," Rachel asked, "where are you going?"

"I gotta go! Bridget needs me!"

Mercy, pale as a sheet, dashed out the door and down the street.

Bridget's house was a few doors down. Mercy breathlessly burst through the door, sucking air like an Olympic sprinter, and looked around frantically for any sign of her friend. No one else was home, and the house was darkened. A handful of night lights cast glowing pools of cold brilliance throughout the dim house.

A terrified whimper wafted from the upstairs bathroom, and Mercy dashed up the stairs. When she reached the top, she froze in her tracks. A thick trail of blood led from Bridget's room, painting a deep scarlet stain along the plush ivory carpet. Bloody towels lay along the hallway, soaked and discarded. Mercy moved slowly, the entire scene too surreal to take in. The hall closed in on her.

With an iron will, she gently pressed the bathroom door. It was like a horror film in slow motion. The door arced open, progressively revealing a scene of terror beyond Mercy's most nightmarish imagination.

Blood was splattered everywhere. Bridget lay in the tub, terrified and crying. Her hands were scarlet and shaking. Crimson handprints were everywhere—the sink, the toilet, the walls. Spatters of blood streaked across the mirror and all over the floor. It looked like the scene of an unimaginable murder, but the victim still lived.

Bridget sat in a puddle of cold bloody water. In her panic, she'd tried to wash the blood off, but she couldn't stem the bleeding.

"It won't stop! Help me!" Bridget cried hysterically.

"What happened?"

"I did it. I didn't want it to ruin my life. They said a baby would ruin my life."

"Oh no!" Mercy wanted to vomit. She was speechless and lightheaded.

"I didn't want it to ruin my life," Bridget cried. "Help me, please."

Tears streamed down Bridget's face, smearing her mascara. With the scarlet smudges on her face, the black streaks made Bridget look like a victim in a monster movie.

"I'm going to call 911."

"No. Don't," Bridget begged. "I don't want my parents to find out."

"Bridget—"

"Call the clinic. They said to call if I needed anything."

"Bridget, please—"

"Call them! The card is on my dresser. Please hurry!"

Mercy rushed to Bridget's bedroom and grabbed the card. With vibrating hands, she fumbled the number into her phone and pressed Send. The wait felt interminable. Finally, a woman answered the line.

"New Dawn Women's Clinic. This is Cindy, how may I help you?"

"My friend is hurt," Mercy blurted.

"I'm sorry. You have the wrong number. Please call 911."

"She won't let me. She went to you today. Now she is bleeding, and it won't stop."

"Please calm down. Nothing is going to happen to her. Bleeding after a procedure is normal and can continue for a few hours. Just put a cold compress on it, and it should stop soon."

"She did that," Mercy insisted, crying, "but there is blood everywhere. It won't stop!"

"Now, now, these things look worse than they are." Cindy tried to calm the terrified caller. "Your friend will be fine."

"I don't think so. Please—we need help."

"Look, if it will make you feel better, I will call the doctor, but I don't think there is anything to worry about. Just give me a few minutes, and I will call you back. What is the number?"

"555-313-2213."

"Just give me five or ten minutes. The doctor should have some ideas."

"OK. Please hurry."

Cindy hung up and dialed the doctor, rapping her nails impatiently on the desk as she waited. After a few rings, the abortionist picked up the phone, irritated and rushed. The call had interrupted his black-tie affair.

"Uh. This isn't a good time," he seethed into the phone.

"This won't take long," Cindy retorted. "A client called in reporting excessive bleeding. This is the third time this week someone had a problem with a procedure you performed."

"It's not like anyone will sue. Have her take two aspirin and call me in the morning."

"Very funny."

"What do you expect me to do?"

"I'm not a doctor," Cindy asserted. "I don't know what to tell her."

"Tell her to get an ice bath and take it easy," he replied, irritation oozing from his lips. "I'll take a look at her on Monday if she really wants that. But I don't do warranty work."

"Well, you'd better *start* if you plan to keep screwing up."

"Look, I've got to go. If she has more trouble, tell her to call 911."

"Thanks for the help," Cindy fired back sarcastically.

She slammed the handset down with an unceremonious bang, then lifted it again to dial the girl. She punched in the number.

Mercy was in the bathroom, trying to calm Bridget and not to get covered in blood herself. She hoped the clinic would offer help that would resolve everything. Once this disaster was over with, they could figure out what to do next.

Mercy jumped as the phone rang. "Hello?"

With a calm, almost saccharin tone, Cindy relayed the abortionist's instructions.

"The doctor suggested taking an ice bath and resting. That should take care of it. Don't worry. Everything will be fine. OK?"

"OK. All right." Mercy tried desperately to get her wits together. "We'll try that. Should I stay on the line?"

"No. It will probably take a few minutes to be effective. Just be patient. OK?"

"OK."

Mercy pressed End and gave Bridget her assurance all would be well.

"I'm getting some ice."

"Please hurry," Bridget urged weakly.

Mercy dashed downstairs to grab the tub from the ice maker. She yanked it from the fridge and rushed upstairs.

Bridget leaned back in the tub. The blood was still streaming, and she squeezed her legs together, hoping that would stem the flow. Mercy dashed in and poured the ice over Bridget.

"Ahh! It's cold."

"She said to be patient."

"I'm sorry. I'm so sorry," Bridget sobbed.

"She said you would be fine," Mercy replied, trying to calm her.

Bridget leaned back in the tub, crying quietly, while Mercy sloshed the ice around.

"It hurts so bad. Oh, God, I'm so sorry. I messed up so bad."

Bridget began to get delirious and to ramble, "Oh, God, forgive me. Please forgive me." She curled up her legs to try to ease the pain. The ice had already become a deep scarlet.

"I feel so tired," she told Mercy, "I'm dizzy. What's happening to me?" Bridget leaned back in the tub, trying for a moment's rest, then darted forward, vomiting on the floor. She'd become ghostly pale, her eyes dilating, and the delirium deepened. Bridget reached out clumsily to find Mercy's hand. Mercy grasped it tightly.

"Does God still love me?"

Mercy began to cry, realization settling in that Bridget was in a dire condition.

"Yes. Yes, He does. Always."

"I was wrong. I'm so sorry." Bridget mustered up a little boost of strength, lifted herself slightly, and looked right into Mercy's eyes. "Don't let me go. Please help me! I think I'm losing it."

Hot, salty tears clouded Mercy's vision as she watched her dearest friend fading before her eyes. She tore herself away from Bridget's grasp so she could reach the phone.

"I am calling again," Mercy blurted, frantically dialing the clinic.

The call went to voicemail.

"I have to call 911."

Bridget was really beginning to lose it. Her skin looked pale, like parchment paper or rice pasta. Her eyes wouldn't focus. She floundered weakly in the tub.

"Please . . . ple . . . help . . . quick . . . help me."

Her terrified pleas trailed off as she passed out.

"No! Bridget! Wake up!"

Mercy frantically punched in the digits. 911. Though it was moments, the wait seemed to take forever.

"911. What is your emergency?"

Sirens blaring and lights flashing, an ambulance screeched to a halt in front of Bridget's home. Mercy met the rescue workers at the door. Just as the 911 operator had told her.

"She's upstairs," Mercy indicated, shock beginning to set in.

Bridget lay in the bathtub, icy water surrounding her and blood covering nearly everything in the room. The paramedics, unsure of what they would find, had brought a variety of tools to triage a patient, but none were prepared for what they saw—and only the veterans of the team were able to zip into action without at least a brief pause at the door. They didn't have time to take in the scene. They had to focus on the injured girl.

A paramedic knelt over her, trying to gage her vital signs. It was crazy action. The men squeezed into a tight place, trying desperately to get a fix on the problem so they could save this girl's life. Within short reach, they had oxygen, a defibrillator, and a drug box. Bandages were in hand, plus tourniquets, scissors, ventilation tubes, ice packs, heat packs, disinfectant spray—dozens of tools to help, but nothing would do any good until they could discover the cause.

"What's going on!? OK, we've got an airway. Respirations are slow and shallow."

After a few moments, they recognized that massive vaginal hemorrhaging was the issue, and they sprang into action.

"We've got intense bleeding, about three units by the look of it."

"Holy . . . What do you need, Dean?"

"Apply pressure. Matt, get a trauma dressing and cold pack, and apply pressure. We have got to stop the bleeding!"

"I've got a carotid at about thirty-five, but no radial."

"Start a line, Stacey. Luke, bag her while I prepare to intubate."

Mercy stood back, sobbing as the paramedics did their work. Dean, the primary paramedic working on Bridget, inserted the tube and cleared her airway. A little vomit gurgled up from the tube. He extracted that and mounted a breathing bag at the end.

Dean performed a sternum rub to see how conscious Bridget was. For those who are fully conscious, the procedure is extremely painful and often elicits a violent response from those who are merely pretending unconsciousness. But from Bridget, he got only a weak groan.

"Young lady," he asked Mercy, "do you know what happened?"

Unable to speak through her tears, she merely handed him the card. As he read New Dawn Women's Clinic, disgust washed over his face, his head shaking in dismay. He backed away as a couple young bucks on the team lifted Bridget from the tub, covered her with a blanket, and strapped her to the gurney.

"Do you know who her doctor is?" Dean asked.

Mercy shook her head.

"Let's go!" one of them shouted.

Dean and Mercy stepped out of the way as they wheeled Bridget by.

"Can I come?"

Patting her shoulder compassionately, Dean shook his head. "No. The police officer will take care of you."

The paramedics hauled the gurney gently but rapidly down the stars and "crashed" her into the ambulance, quickly folding the wheels out of the way. They leaped in and locked everything down.

Just then, Clayton and Rachel arrived. They were concerned when Mercy dashed out of the house and had practically panicked when, twenty minutes later, an ambulance wheeled up to Bridget's door. They'd rushed over just in time to meet it.

Clayton reached for the door handle of the ambulance, but the police officer prevented his entry.

"I'm sorry, sir, but only authorized personnel may be here."

"I am the medical director, officer," Clayton replied, flashing his ID.

He opened the door and stepped into the ambulance, then turned to Rachel. "Meet us at the ER."

He closed and latched the door.

"Oh, glad you're here, Doc. Let's go!" Dean replied.

Moments later, the bulky vehicle, full lights and sirens, hurled its way toward the nearest emergency room.

The ER was quiet—like a deep calm before a violent storm. Urgent triage cases, such as this one, only happened a couple times a week, but when they did, it was all-hands-on-deck.

A silver-haired nurse—usually pleasant, but all business now—met the emergency crew at the ambulance dock. "Guys! Take her to room six. Dr. Morris is on his way."

"We'll need three units of type A-negative whole blood," Dr. Patterson ordered. "Thank you, Maude."

The team rushed the gurney to room 6, a variety of specialists surrounding it and trying to complete or prepare their various tasks.

"Guys," Clayton ordered, "let's get good documentation on this. Let me know when you're finished with the emergency report. I'd like to see it."

Dr. Morris entered the triage room. Though dressed for business, his Rolex still glittered from beneath his smock. He donned his cap and mask and approached the gurney.

"What do we have?" Dr. Morris asked.

"Internal bleeding," Dr. Patterson replied. "Here is the chart."

Alarms sounded, and the monitor beeped erratically, showing unstable and fading vitals. A nurse arrived with an infusion, leaping into the frantic fray as medical professionals of all stripes worked to save this girl's life.

Rachel and Mercy sat, hugging, in the waiting room. Waiting seemed like such an inappropriate word for that space. Those who merely waited were just passing the time, and it went along pleasantly and quickly enough. But those trapped in this room were not waiting. They were hoping. And the wait seemed ever so long—far longer than, by the clock, it truly was.

But what does a clock know?

Suddenly the double doors burst open and two frantic middle-aged people rushed in. They flew over to the reception desk in a state of panic.

Alerted by the noise, Mercy and Rachel looked up to see Martin and Nancy, Bridget's parents. Rachel went to meet them at the counter.

"We are Bridget Matthews's parents," Martin told the duty nurse. "We want to see our daughter."

"Drs. Patterson and Morris are with her now," she replied, "I will inform them that you are here."

She darted out to the treatment area. Rachel opened her arms to Nancy. The distraught mother fell into her embrace. Rachel tried to calm and encourage her. "Come, Nancy. They just brought her in."

"Oh dear! Martin, we shouldn't have left her alone."

"Nancy, we need to trust God now," Rachel comforted her. "We need to know that, somehow, Bridget will be all right."

An ER nurse poked her head through the door and asked for the Matthews family.

"We are here, ma'am," Martin replied.

"If you come with me, Dr. Morris will speak with you now."

Minutes later, Martin and Nancy slipped back into the waiting room.

It was still quiet. A calm buzz continued its reign through the space. The clock still ticked off its time. The magazines still glittered colorfully from the tables. The ads still played on the monitor.

But all Mercy could see were the Matthews. They shuffled toward her sightlessly, arm in arm. Martin was stunned and Nancy tearful. Mercy knew immediately what had happened.

Bridget was dead.

The world had ended.

CHAPTER TEN

Nightmare

You could hear a pin drop.

The audience was stunned. Women covered their quivering lips with their hands, holding their breaths as if they would be their last. Men smudged salty drops from their moist eyes.

Years of policy debates, sex-ed classes, posters, and ads had convinced them that this sort of thing didn't happen anymore. They believed it was ancient history—part of the back-rooms-and-coat-hangers world before *Roe v. Wade*. Certainly, most thought, with modern medical abortion, perfect safety had been established.

Now, before their eyes glared the horrible truth. Some, for a split second, imagined their own daughters suffering like that. Others recalled the secret, nightmarish experiences of their own pasts. Nearly everyone had bent their hearts toward Mercy and her grief.

Mercy sobbed inconsolably. Though wrapped like a young child in her mother's arms, her grief was very grown-up and agonizing. She was lost in regret, wishing she had done something—anything—that might have helped her friend in time. Rachel was in tears too, dearly missing the angel she so vividly remembered and trying desperately to comfort her daughter.

Tears clouded Rene's eyes as well, feeling every regret and self-remonstration pouring from the lips of this broken teen girl.

"I'm so sorry, Mercy," Rene commiserated. "I truly understand why you feel so strongly about this."

Parker, on the other hand, sat arms crossed in stoic silence. Reading his response to the news was difficult. Though he didn't know the details, his association with the senator and their mutual efforts for causes had put him inside "the circle." He was somewhat aware of the situation, but despite his best attempts to avert it, had just watched the story stream out before an audience of millions. Parker fully supported the senator's pro-choice efforts. While he sympathized with Mercy's sorrow, he felt that abortion was an inalienable right.

Cindy raged, her world—even her very existence—seemed threatened. She lost her usual self-possessed control and, trying desperately to win the audience back, virtually exploded with a rambling diatribe. "That's not what happens! The procedures are safer than giving birth. They give women their lives back. For you to sit there and say that this one incident is what happens to every woman is ignorant. It's extreme. You don't really care about women. You just want to keep them barefoot and pregnant." Anger and frustration painted Cindy's features crimson. "Haven't you heard what I am saying?! I know what it's really like. I had an abortion, and it was the best decision I ever made!"

Parker and Rene turned their full attention toward Cindy. The audience had not yet processed the announcement, but the hosts fathomed the import of Cindy's revelation. The words hung in the air for a moment, then the stone-silent crowd began to buzz, sweeping like a wave across the studio.

Cindy finally had everyone's attention.

The purr of the engine shuddered to a stop. A much younger Cindy, only about twenty, paused in her seat, indecision weighing her down. Right before her stood the entrance to New Dawn Women's Clinic. Just yards away was the door that would change her life (she hoped) for the better, but her fears said otherwise. The weight of the decision pressed her deeply into her seat and stole her breath away.

Cindy appeared to have everything going for her. Her family was prominent in the state and quite wealthy. Her alma mater was an exclusive private college of which her family had been eternal patrons. She drove a sporty Jaguar XKR convertible, a cherry little ride that grabbed the attention of the hottest boys on campus.

One in particular had taken a fancy to her, and their romance sparked hot and heavy. Captain on the football team and top dog in his fraternity, Geo Rayburns was tons of fun. Coming from a family that owned half the auto dealerships in the state, he was a shoo-in for approval from her father. To top it all, he was drop-dead gorgeous—a perfect match for the hot blond poly-sci major who just happened to be the most popular chick in school.

But Geo wasn't the serious type. He just liked to kid around and party up. He certainly enjoyed the bedroom action, but hey, he was "all that," so why not soak in the attention of all the coed's who'd thrown themselves at him? He was a "third semester" Sophomore, expecting to carve out at least two more years of partying before he faced the firing squad of real life.

Cindy, on the other hand, couldn't afford to take life as a joke. She had to prove herself to her father—a man with inaccessibly high expectations, the first of which was that she should have been a boy. He expected that she would be a brilliant Kewpie Doll—perfect in every way and museum grade. If her report contained a single *A*, she would be lambasted that it hadn't been an *A+*. If she played just one wrong note in a Rachmaninov symphony, her father would hear it—then she'd "hear it" for hours the next day. Nothing was ever good enough. Perfection was the only option. There was a name to live up to.

His name.

Having just come from a student-body event, Cindy still sported her preppy uniform in collegiate colors. The school was exclusive enough that, even at the turn of the century, the students all wore uniforms. Sitting there, looking at the New Dawn storefront, she realized that she couldn't enter while wearing the school uniform. Someone might see. She peeled off the sweater, leaving only the white collared button-up she wore underneath. The skirt was a pleated charcoal gray, a common-enough style that she hoped no one would notice.

Cindy scanned the parking lot. Having taken the last available spot in the minuscule lot—she was in the perfect position to clearly see both the entrance to the clinic and the marquee of the neighboring church—New Life Community Church. It was almost as if the two choices lay before her like forked trails. The moment she took one path, the other would be forever closed to her.

She sighed deeply.

Suddenly, a cramp hit her in the gut like a steel boot. She cried out in pain. As suddenly as it hit, it was gone. She was nervous, even shaking.

For a split second, she wondered if there was any way back—if she still had time to choose.

She was already showing, though she'd done a great job of hiding the pregnancy. She had secretly hoped that the baby would free her from her father's grip, giving her a shot at freedom—and maybe even a real life. She'd almost been home free, in fact, but a chance slip of the tongue alerted him. Seven months in, he'd found out.

She laid her head back in her seat, hot, steaming tears moistening her eyes. She squeezed them shut, recalling the fiery words her father had vomited like volcanic lava.

"Cynthia Pierce Stevens!! We wouldn't have had this problem if you were a boy!" he'd screamed. "Do you know what the voters would do if they found out you are pregnant? How could you do this to me? You're a Stevens. It's about time you started acting like one!

"Go down to the clinic and get this taken care of. I'll set it up for you. I'm not going to let this mess ruin me!"

The tears began to roll as her mind shifted from that agonizing moment to the reality check her roommate had given her.

"You don't really think Geo'd marry you just because you're pregnant?" she'd asked sarcastically.

Cindy knew the answer. In fact, knowing Geo, he was probably seducing some bright-eyed freshman at this very moment.

Her tears came with convulsions as realization hit her. Geo's own words seared through her heart. Sure, she pretended that she was a modern liberated woman, but deep in her soul, she'd wanted him to say something completely different. She'd wanted him to say she mattered above everything—the first and only person in her life who'd have expressed that. But those weren't the words she got.

"Come on, Cindy!" Geo had chided. "Don't be an idiot! We can't get married right now! I'd lose my scholarship. Look, just take care of it, and we can get back to the way things were."

Another cramp snapped her back to the present moment. She took a deep, tired breath and scrubbed the tears from her eyes. The church marquee suddenly lit up, as if a bad fluorescent lamp finally chose to work. The flash caught her attention, and the words on the sign seared into her soul.

JESUS DIED FOR YOUR SINS. YOUR BABY DOES NOT HAVE TO.

The pain turned to fury. It all seemed so unfair. If God really cared, why would he have put her with such a prick of a father and made her love a boy who didn't even know what love was. She just wanted to lash out at anything and everything.

"It's my life, God!" Cindy shouted, "My choice!"

Cindy stepped up to the counter in the clinic. She felt subdued, and everything seemed foreign. Yes, this was her father's clinic, but she didn't really feel that she belonged. It seemed like a foreign world. Senator Stevens might have owned the clinic, but it wasn't politically expedient for that fact to be generally known, so he almost never set foot in the facility, and she didn't either. It was just not discussed—like a dirty secret of practical politics.

"Hi. I'm back for my second appointment," she told the receptionist.

"Sign in, please."

With a quick dash, Cindy signed some unintelligible autograph that, quite intentionally, did not resemble her own. The receptionist confirmed that payment had been made then slid a couple forms toward her. She scribbled her signature on the release form—a sheet acknowledging certain symptoms or conditions she might encounter following her procedure—and glanced over the post-op checklist.

"Have a seat in the waiting area," the receptionist said, "and your counselor will be with you when she is available."

"Thank you," Cindy responded uncertainly, but the receptionist had already turned back to her work.

The lobby chairs were cheap but adequately padded, and a single end table sat along the wall between a pair of them. Various pro-choice flyers were carefully arranged around a colorful fake plant. Even a few copies of *Globe*, *Esquire*, and *Ebony* magazines rested on the table, calling out to be read by nervous girls trying to pass the time. The lobby was lit by two industrial fluorescent fixtures, peeking through tiles in the drop ceiling, that cast a faint green pall. In some subconscious way, Cindy felt that even the lobby looked like death.

She took a seat and was immediately hit with another cramp. She tried her best not to cry out and startle others in the facility. As the pain passed, she noticed another bit of drama quietly unfolding across the room.

Dressed as a nurse, a counselor sat next to an angry, scared young woman. She seemed to be about fourteen or fifteen and appeared to disagree animatedly with the counselor. A gentleman, old enough to be her father, though very obviously not, sat next to her on the opposite side. In the counselor's hand was a clipboard with forms that she was adamantly trying to convince the girl to sign.

Cindy couldn't help overhearing the discussion.

"Listen, we came all this way," the man commented. "You can at least hear what she has to say."

"You're what, fourteen, maybe fifteen?" the counselor asked.

"Fifteen next week," the girl responded.

"Can you imagine," the counselor asked sympathetically, "how it would be for you to be a mom at fifteen? While your friends are out having fun, you'd be stuck at home. And then there's college. Going to school is stressful enough without having to chase a toddler around. Trust me. I've been to college."

"I don't care. I won't kill my baby," the girl insisted.

"Listen. We can talk about your options privately. For right now, please just complete this paperwork so we can handle your medical records properly."

"But all these forms talk about *abortion*. I didn't come here for that. I just want to make sure my baby is all right."

"But a baby would ruin your life," the man responded.

"Or yours!" the girl retorted, glaring savagely at him.

He got rather nervous and red in the face.

"Don't . . . You can't . . . You . . ." he stammered.

The counselor held her hand up like a traffic cop, and he stopped midsentence. But instead of asking more on the subject, or even chiding him for what seemed like a possible indiscretion, she addressed the girl.

"What we are trying to do," she asserted matter-of-factly, "is help you make the best decision you can make in these circumstances. We care about you. These forms do talk about abortion because that is an option you have, and that procedure is available here, and we have to have all our patients sign the same paperwork. Just complete the forms. We'll have the doctor do a prenatal examination, and then we can discuss what options you have."

"It's all for the best," the man began, but the counselor cut him off again.

"Once the paperwork is done, please bring it to me, and I will get you into the next available exam room, OK?"

The young woman seemed unsure, but she finally began to sign the forms. The counselor stepped away as the youth worked on her paperwork, and the gentleman seemed to relax a little. But he kept a keen eye on her to make sure all was done properly.

The examination room was rather dim and chilly. Not freezing, like an icebox. Just cool. But to a girl in a hospital gown, that was plenty cold. A single fluorescent fixture lit the room. Next to the examination table, however, an articulating arm supported a brilliant spotlight, much like that beside a dentist's chair, so the abortionist could get a good light on the subject. A roll-away table, arranged with instruments on a blue surgical drop cloth, rested next to the storm-gray cinderblock wall. Next to the exit door, a small, plain supply cabinet was permanently fixed. A few handy items, like swabs and gauze, were arranged in useful piles.

The examination table was adjustable, moving from flat to reclined, and featured metal stirrups that allowed the patient to hold her legs widely apart for the several minutes each procedure took.

The lead nurse was the only person in the vacant room. She was graying, slightly plump, and maintained an inscrutable countenance. Her pencil scratched rapidly on the clipboard she held in her hand.

The door cracked almost noiselessly, and a timid young teen crept into the room. She closed the door behind her and looked around furtively. A second door, leading to the main office area, remained closed. On it hung a whiteboard with initials and a variety of scratches and lines that could have as easily been Chinese as anything else.

The nurse looked up from her clipboard, and noticing the girl's hesitation, waved her over. With a wordless gesture, she indicated that the girl should climb aboard the exam table. The youngster complied as the nurse returned to her form. Once completed, the nurse refocused on the girl.

"All right," she said, "the doctor will come in shortly to examine you. It should not be long."

"I'm scared." The quivering girl panted a little in trepidation.

The attendant patted the girl's hand. "There's nothing to it," the nurse assured with a tired smile. "Everything will be fine."

She stepped toward the second exit, clapping the clipboard onto the counter on her way out, and pulled the door closed behind her. It latched with a click that seemed to echo loudly with a cold finality.

The counseling room was hardly different than it would be in a dozen years. The only differences were the brochures and posters. Absent the flashy graphics and full-color photos of women smiling, crisp two-color printing on classy ivory brochure paper boldly described the benefits of choosing the clinic's services.

Cindy perused the flyers as she awaited the return of her counselor. After a few minutes, the counselor returned, clipboard in hand.

"All right, Ms."—she checked the clipboard—"Smith. It's been forty-eight hours. You say you are now cramping?"

"Yes," Cindy replied.

"OK. We'll get you into an exam room. Everything should be good-to-go for completing the procedure."

The counselor guided Cindy through a long, barren corridor. No artwork, posters, or decorations lined the stone-gray walls. The only thing breaking up the monotony of the walk were pools of light from the industrial fluorescent bulbs. The pair arrived at a door, and the counselor motioned for Cindy to enter.

"Here. There are gowns stacked in the closet. Please put one on, then I will take you to the examination room once it's your turn."

A little voice in the back of Cindy's mind wondered if it was too late to turn back. A wave of dread passed through her body, but she fought back the feeling and silenced the voice. She insisted to herself she was doing the right thing.

Cindy entered the room, softly closing the door behind her.

Down the hallway, the abortionist had arrived and stepped into the exam room where the young woman was waiting.

The door closed with a thump that startled the girl. She rose up from the exam table to see that the abortionist and two nurses had entered the room. This young abortionist, freshly minted from medical school, was looking forward to a long, lucrative career. Though dressed differently from his dandy tux, Dr. Morris's steel eyes peeked from behind his hygienic mask and surgical cap to survey the situation. The nurse who had greeted him trailed him to the exam, table along with a young, somewhat tentative intern.

Her first day on the job, the intern was still rather shell shocked by the reality of what happened at the clinic. Almost mindlessly, she followed the orders given by the older nurse.

The doctor did not peruse the chart, ask questions, or even request the girl's name. He simply set to work.

"All right. Just lay back and relax. This will not take long."

"You are just doing a—a prenatal exam, right?" she asked.

"Certainly," he replied offhandedly. "Now lay back."

The intern slid a stool to the proper spot and positioned the searing light to give the abortionist a clear view. The girl leaned back and took a ragged nervous breath.

Deep inside the caressing folds of her womb, a tiny infant nestled, sleeping and sucking his thumb. Small enough to fit into the palm of one's hand, his fragile figure was practically transparent, revealing an intricate network of scarlet blood vessels. His tiny heart beat quickly—almost at the rate of machine-gun fire—rushing life-giving nutrients to the farthest reaches of his rapidly growing body. His fingers, fully formed, clenched in cute little fists. A soothing echo of his young mother's heartbeat rang through the viscous liquid in which he swam, slept, and dreamed. He knew her voice, heard music, and took in the dim, muddled noise of the world outside. When she slept, he would wake and sport about like the energetic little man he would become, but small as he was, she could feel only the slightest tickle from his Olympic antics. But when she was awake, her living motion lulled him into a restful sleep. And that's how we found him as she lay on the exam table.

The faint sounds of a small, quiet vacuum cleaner powered up. Wholly unfamiliar with the normal process of a prenatal exam, the girl accepted the noise as a common part of the experience. She tried to brush away the nagging nervousness that accompanied her visit to this strange, cold place.

The nurse stepped around behind the bed and took a firm—almost iron—grip on her shoulders, pinning her down.

"You need to be still for this," she said gently, trying to convey her concern through her exhaustion. "Otherwise, you may get hurt." She extended her wrinkled, aging hand to the girl's. "If the pressure gets too intense, just squeeze my hand. You'll be all right."

Suddenly, an agonizing pain seared through her abdomen. Panic suddenly rose in her heart, and she struggled against the agony. "What are you doing!?" she screamed.

Though efforts had been made to prevent unsettling noises from drifting down the hallway and into the ears of other already nervous patients, the outcry couldn't be fully contained. Cindy, just a couple doors down the hall, overheard the girl's exclamation. Instinctively she cracked the door to hear, in more clarity, what was going on.

"Lay back, or you could die," Cindy heard the abortionist say, his words muddied by the closed door. "I will be done in a moment,"

"I didn't come here for this!" the girl cried in response.

"Shhh," the nurse pressed earnestly. "Please lay back. This is for the best. Everything will be all right, OK? Just hold on to me."

The girl gazed readily into the nurse's eyes and squeezed her hand. The tired woman tried not to wince from the pain. From the room, Cindy could hear only the faint sound of suction.

Cindy took a sharp breath and closed the door, doing her best to make no sound. She leaned against it, almost in a subconscious effort to prevent entry by an intruder. She wanted to flee.

But she had no choice.

She took a deep breath and closed her eyes, battling fiercely to calm herself and carry on.

Inside the exam room, the young lady lay, shaking violently as tears streamed down her cheeks. Every motion of the abortionist sent new waves of agony coursing through her body, and she fought desperately not to leap from the table and dash away.

Inside the comforting sanctum of her womb, a large, needle-like projectile inched toward the sleeping infant. Linked to the powerful sucking machine, it drew in some amniotic fluid, but it wasn't designed to empty the fluid from the amniotic sac. No, it had a more sinister purpose. Just as a child playing with a vacuum hose might stick the hose onto her arm or leg by force of the suction, this tube was designed to stick to the limbs and organs of an unborn child. Unlike the toddler, however, who finds it harmless child's play, this this instrument was lethal.

The abortionist, blindly probing with no ultrasound or other way to guide his movements with precision, poked the sleeping infant. The child awoke with a start and began frantically swimming away from the painful protrusion. An expression of horror—a look any mother could recognize—flashed across his delicate face. Like any small child in pain, he screamed, but the heavy viscous fluid—which only moments before felt comforting, warm, and safe—drowned any sound he could have made.

Again and again the tube poked at him. Finally, it latched on firmly. The abortionist did a twist and pull. The connection wasn't solid, but it was firm enough to yank a hefty piece of flesh from his buttocks. His little arms and legs waved desperately in a vain attempt to get away.

The abortionist pulled the probe from the girl's vagina. A small piece of flesh, obviously from the baby, was stuck to it. A look of satisfaction glinted from his eyes. He had successfully found the infant. He held the tissue over a cold stainless tray and deftly pressed a small button on the side of the handle. The extraction machine made a new sound as the vacuum bypassed the probe and the bloody buttocks fell noiselessly into the tray.

Again, the abortionist inserted the probe. Again, he poked around. Again, it stuck firmly onto the frail body of the little boy. Again, the abortionist twisted and pulled. This time the prize was bigger. The move wrenched the lad's entire leg from his body. Blood poured from the wound, clouding the amniotic fluid in crimson. In utter agony and terror, he twisted and turned, but escape was not an option.

The abortionist extracted the leg, just as he had that first bit of flesh. It was clinical. Mechanical. There wasn't even a twitch or flutter in his expression as he examined the grotesque, disfigured limb. Again, he dropped it into the tray and reinserted the probe. He worked quickly, with a practiced hand, almost as if he were racing a clock.

The infant was faltering. The probe latched onto an arm. With a horrific twist and pull, it too was gone. The translucent body paled, nearly drained of its blood. The heart slowed.

Then all was still.

The only sound that remained was the horrible sucking sound.

Piece by piece, the abortionist extracted the minuscule components of the lifeless little boy. Each part lay in the tray, adding up little by little to the tragic end of a brief existence.

Once satisfied that he cleared everything, he backed away and signaled that the patient should go. The graying nurse helped the girl off the exam table as the intern unfolded a wheelchair. The poor young lady, looking dazed and pale, simply slumped lifelessly in the wheelchair.

Blood covered much of the exam table, the floor, and the abortionist's disposable smock. Throwing his final instructions over his shoulder, he headed for the other exit so he could change. "Reset. And be quick about it. You can't take ten minutes like the last time. You've got five."

The old nurse sighed, exhaustion dripping from her weary frame and rolled the girl out the main door toward the recovery room, but the intern, as if on autopilot, complied and began hurriedly cleaning up the mess.

The old wheelchair clicked rhythmically as a nursing assistant wheeled Cindy down the barren hallway. Another cramp shot arrows of agony through her body. Cindy pressed her hands onto her stomach where the pain seared most deeply and cried out instinctively.

The heavy steel door creaked as the assistant rolled Cindy into the exam room. The old nurse and the young intern were just completing their reset. A fresh white cloth covered the exam bed, replacing the linens soiled only moments ago. The floor had been mopped, and the sharp odor of Lysol and bleach filled the cramped space.

The assistant and the nurse helped Cindy up onto the table. She leaned back, uncertainty still ringing through her mind.

The nurse ordered the assistant to begin the drip. Deftly, the IV tower was rolled next to Cindy, the Oxytocin bag hung, and a shunt inserted. It all happened in a flash.

The assistant motioned to the intern. "Set this to twenty drips per minute."

The intern complied, the dial clicking as she rotated it to twenty. Clear liquid began to drop rapidly into the receiver and course into Cindy's veins.

Curious, the intern asked, "And this does?"

"It induces labor," the nurse noted.

After a few moments, a walloping cramp stole Cindy's breath. She instinctively gritted her teeth. A deep groan rumbled through her body as she twisted with the agony, trying to draw her legs up to relieve the pain. The nurse and the assistant gripped tightly, holding her firmly in place.

"Don't squirm," the nurse ordered. "You'll pull out the drip." To the intern, she added, "Here. Have her hold your hand and just squeeze when a cramp hits, OK?"

The intern offered her hand and Cindy gave it a crushing squeeze. The young woman winced but took the pain like a trooper.

When the cramp subsided, Cindy was shaking and weak. Beads of cold sweat gushed from her pale forehead, and she panted, desperately trying to catch her breath. Like a mantra, she repeated one thought through her head, hoping to calm herself and make it through.

"It will be over soon. It will be over soon . . ."

Cindy relaxed somewhat, and the nurse stepped around to check her progress. A deep frown scrawled across her features and she shook her head.

For about ten minutes, this process repeated itself—each cramp worse than the last—the nausea, the exhaustion, and the frown. Each wave must only have been a minute or two apart, but to Cindy each seemed like an eternity.

Finally, the interminable cycle ended with a few clipped words. "Four centimeters," the nurse observed. "Crowning. She's ready."

The assistant stepped out the door, returning moments later with the abortionist. He was, again, dressed in a smock, cap, and mask. All was clean and ready to go.

He took his seat on the stool and checked Cindy's progress. Not satisfied, he shot out a terse command. "We need to get this thing moving. Bump to forty."

"Go to forty," the nurse ordered the intern.

Again, complying swiftly, the intern rotated the dial. Suddenly, Cindy felt as if she'd been punched in the gut.

Sometimes doctors will ask patients to rate their pain on a scale of ten—zero being pain free and ten being unbearable. When Cindy had broken her collar bone as a child, she'd have rated that a ten.

This cramp instantly demoted that pain to a four.

She couldn't hold back the tears. Though too proud to sob, Cindy cried quietly, her face twisted in agony.

This cramp seemed to hold on forever. It stole her breath away and kept it. She couldn't even move. Little sparkles began to flood about in her darkening sight, and she felt as if she were in a tunnel.

Finally, the cramp subsided—only to be followed by another more powerful contraction. Her groan, more like a scream and cry, echoed in the cave-like chamber.

"Keep her quiet!" the abortionist ordered.

"Anesthesia?" The nurse asked.

"No. It would only slow things down. We need to get this done."

Bewildered and alone, Cindy was racked with mind-numbing pain.

"What's happening? They never said it would hurt like this," she panted desperately, her reddened face wet with tears.

"Imagine a *real* delivery, honey," the nurse replied comfortingly. "This ain't nothin'."

The cramps hit one upon another. Without breath, Cindy could only writhe spasmodically.

"OK. Here it comes," the abortionist noted. "Get the bag ready."

He sounded clinical—distant—to Cindy. The cold detachment in his tone clashed with the waves of agony that coursed through her body, much like discordant, angry music.

She couldn't understand.

The intern stood back, taking in the specter. Overwhelmed, she almost felt as if she were watching the whole scene through a grimy movie screen. Everything seemed slower than life—and heavy, like the momentous scene in a horror film.

It was her first day on the job and no one had prepared her for what it was really like. From everything she'd heard about the process growing up, she'd almost expected teddy bears and cotton candy. She knew that wasn't realistic. This was a medical facility. But she wasn't prepared for the blood, the crying, and the screams.

The screams—

The nurse got her attention. "That's you!" she ordered urgently.

The intern swung into motion. Her arms and legs were loaded with lead. Every word—every sound—echoed cavernously within her ears. With an effort, she rushed to the cabinet and pulled a biohazard bag from beneath the counter. As she turned to the abortionist, everything seemed to go into super slow motion.

Something went wrong.

Cindy's body convulsed violently. Her scarlet face tinged blue, and locked teeth parted to release a gurgling scream. The world swam before her eyes, and she passed out.

The intern found herself right next to the abortionist without being certain how she got there. A little bald head was breaking through Cindy's cervix. The abortionist glanced away, reaching for forceps to crush the skill and pull the lifeless "parasite" from Cindy's body. In that moment, a small motion vibrated the patient's pelvis, and suddenly the little cap became a full head. Eyes, ears, nose, mouth. With a burst of passion, the little one broke out upon an unsuspecting world, screaming her little lungs out. Her arms flailed in emphasis as she landed full on in the abortionist's hand.

"What the . . ." he shouted in shock.

Time stood still. Everyone froze in their places. The inexperienced abortionist was livid. He had failed his procedure. His mind whirled like a tornado, dizzying him with a myriad of options and potential consequences.

The nurse stood thunderstruck at the utterly unimaginable situation. She had never seen a child emerge alive from a saline abortion and had never known an instance wherein the abortionist had failed to guarantee termination with the forceps. She had no idea what to do.

The intern, on the other hand, had quite a different set of thoughts. Trained as a nurse and possessing the motherly instincts most women hold, she suddenly realized that this little one was a baby. Through all her training, she'd been taught that this was a *fetus*, a lump of tissue, akin to a benign tumor or a parasite. She had been told that it was not a baby, and terminating it was a fundamental human right. But as she, through her shock and dismay, looked on that minuscule screaming, squirming little girl, everything she'd been told rang hollow.

The abortionist was the first to come to some semblance of his senses and snapped the room back into reality. He'd landed on a solution—*pass the buck*. Angrily, he chucked the infant to the intern and smartly clipped the umbilical cord.

"Take care of it!" he barked, rising from his stool.

The intern gazed at this little one—nearly the size of any newborn—that filled her two gloved hands. Uncertainty coursed through her mind.

"You've got to be kidding me," he muttered under his breath as he stormed for the door. His latex gloves landed in the trash can with a distinct *thwack*, and the door slammed loudly.

The reanimated nurse began shaking and calling to Cindy to awaken her. They needed her to finish her labor and expel the placenta before moving her to recovery, and she had to be awake for that. The intern remained statuesquely in place, locked in uncertainty. The tired old nurse realized the intern had done nothing and hurriedly waved her out of the room.

The intern found her legs and rushed from the room, the crying baby squirming frantically. Behind her, a groggy moan escaped the closing door as Cindy regained consciousness.

The door crashed open as Cindy, once again riding the ancient wheelchair, was steered into the recovery room. A couple of other exhausted patients glanced up lethargically from their beds. The young woman Cindy had heard in the room before her, however, made no motion. She faced the wall, sobbing deeply and quietly, despair enveloping her. The assistant helped Cindy move into the bed so she could rest before leaving.

The counselor entered the room with a tray of orange juice and ibuprofen. She stepped to the distraught teen. "Here's something to help."

In an explosion of fury, the youth slapped the cup from her hand. Juice striped across the wall nearby and stained the sheets on an unoccupied bed. The cup made a loud clatter as it bounced and rebounded across the floor. "You lied to me!" she screamed through her tears.

"It was for the best," the counselor retorted.

Deflated, the young woman lay back and faced the wall, silent and spent. She felt like a zombie. Dead. Hollow inside. Her tears no longer came. She just lay there.

Frustrated and impatient, the counselor turned to Cindy. "Here's something to help," she repeated mechanically.

Dazed and exhausted, Cindy accepted the proffered items silently, shakily popped the pills past her lips, and sipped the juice, careful of the nausea swirling in her bowels.

The counselor left the room, and Cindy leaned back gingerly into the bed until her head rested on the pillow. Within a few brief minutes, she lapsed into a fitful and uneasy sleep.

Twigs snapped. Rocks scattered. Branches grabbed. Thorns pierced.

Rapid steps raced down the path.

Tears streaming. Gown tearing.

Terror menacing like a midnight panther.

Tears fogged her eyes—clouding the small form that fled in the distance. Terrified cries pierced the darkness.

In a room not far away, the squirmy little infant lay on a cold counter, bright fluorescent lights stinging her tender eyes. She cried lustily, far more loudly than you'd expect from such a little thing. Her fists clenched tightly as she shivered and screeched.

Chasing. Ever chasing.

Heart pounding. Fear mounting.

It was too late. It was too late!

Realization overwhelming.

The distant figure grew close—yet ever out of reach.

Branches wrapped their tentacles around her, shredding the nightgown and obscuring the weeping little form that dashed helter-skelter before her.

The intern mindlessly tussled through a stack of clean towels, fishing for the perfect one for the job. Her mind raced and heart pounded. The flailing arms flashed in the corner of her eye, making it difficult to focus on the task at hand.

Her stomach churned as she settled on one neatly folded, fluffy cloth. Through her blue latex gloves, the looped threads of the terry cloth weave felt like thousands of tiny fingers. Her mind wandered to images of those infinitesimal little fingers—perfect microscopic copies of her own. With an effort, she shoved the thoughts out of her mind and steeled herself to the task at hand.

Darkness—panther-like—pursued. Horror filled her marrow.

Bushes and briars rose into terrifying fiends. The midnight specter screamed into a breathless wind—its howls flooding shivers of hopelessness.

The fleeing figure fell. Crying. Terrified. Her shouts for help were muddled and distant. Piercing. Unintelligible.

Cindy couldn't understand the words—but she felt the fear as if it were her own.

Thorns stabbed like razor blades. She dashed onward— reaching, grasping, hardly daring to hope.

Sliding. Kicking. Ripping.

She reached the crevasse into which the little figure fell. The white gown, muddied by the fall, flailed and flowed with the child's every frantic move.

She couldn't see the face, but somehow, she knew.

Reaching. Stretching.

She slipped into the channel. Gripping. Pulling.

The trees themselves fought against her, their powerful limbs suspending her above the panicked little lass.

Inches. Just inches away.

She couldn't reach.

Cries pierced the darkness.

The intern soaked the towel in cold water. The war within her soul waged more fiercely than any she'd ever encountered. Almost as if motivated by a force outside of her, she moved mechanically to the counter and suspended the sopping towel over the fragile scarlet figure.

It would be fast, she told herself. It would be painless, she told herself. Just a few moments under the towel and the cries would stop forever.

The dark terror crashed onward. The trees parted and shook—as if shuddering at the horror themselves.

Too late! Too late!! The thoughts coursed through her limbs like electricity.

Only inches. Too far.

A reach. A stretch. Their fingers touched.

Then darkness was upon them.

A scream of utter terror. Despair. Hopelessness.

Silence. Only gut-wrenching silence.

It was too late.

Cindy woke with a start. Sobs tore through her aching body, hot tears flowing such as she'd never cried before. The world swam before her. She couldn't tell if she was awake in the horrible real world or locked in the terrifying nightmare.

No one came to comfort her.

The intern stood over the body of the little one. Wicked red acid burns wrinkled and scarred her delicate skin. A deep wound raced up her left arm, resembling an evil scarlet lightning bolt.

The intern hesitated. This felt like a bridge too far.

The arms and legs waved in frantic, desperate motion. The infant's toothless mouth was spread wide like a trumpet, loudly declaring her pain and fear.

Thoughts of her past, present, and future swirled through the intern's mind. She had entered the nursing profession to help people and save lives. Her mother always felt that lost causes were noble, and that people mattered.

She'd taken the position because she ardently believed that accessible abortion was a human right—ranking up there with life and liberty. She was as feminist as any liberated collegiate woman and she passionately wanted to stand with the causes of women everywhere.

The intern's mind wandered—in an instant—to her future. She needed this job and experience. If she didn't do this, she'd lose both. Then what would her mother say?

But could she live with herself if she did? Tumors didn't scream; they didn't wave their arms. Parasites didn't resemble their hosts in body, mind, and soul.

Offspring did.

Children didn't suck life from their species. They perpetuated its existence.

She recalled a professor's declaration that abortion was a fundamental part of women's healthcare—that denying choice to a woman was at its core an attack on her humanity and self-determination. The intern had even denounced— loudly—those in her class who had dared to disagree.

But writhing before her lay this little girl, one whose very existence was discounted by the intern's mentors. And she'd seriously considered snuffing out this little woman's life in the name of women's rights.

How could she betray everything she'd ever stood for by defending everything she'd ever believed in?

With fiery mental anguish, the intern slowly lowered the dripping towel over the infant.

Suddenly, the little bit grabbed ahold of the intern's finger, grasping it tightly, and stopped crying. The intern froze. She looked into the fathomless black eyes, feeling the cloudy gaze that they returned. The grip was surprisingly firm. The nurse-to-be couldn't help inspecting the little fingers that held her own. All but one was perfect. The horrid burn had carved its way up the arm, across the wrist, and along the pinky finger, badly distorting the tiny digit.

Time stood still.

The world suddenly became crystal clear. The weight lifted, and Rachel knew what she must do. She ripped off her mask, wrapped the infant protectively in a dry towel, and dashed for the exit door.

CHAPTER ELEVEN

Undone

The stage lights shone like a row of fiery suns scorching the guests with their searing heat. The air had been sucked from the room. The silence was deafening. No one dared breathe.

No one could believe what they'd just heard. Astonishment painted its way across every face in the room. All but one. Even Parker was speechless. Rene's throat tightened, choking off any word she was inclined to say. Rachel was tearful. Mercy was white as a sheet, holding a death grip on the armrests.

Of all people in the room, Senator Stevens was the only one who seemed not to be surprised. His arms crossed and his jaw set, he showed not the slightest hint of change or emotion. His practiced poker face remained intact.

He alone had known of Mercy's survival. He alone knew that the intern had fled with that "hazardous biowaste." He alone had received the attorney who'd represented the intern. He alone, as the senator and attorney, had negotiated the closed adoption that promised to dispose of this mess forever. None but he knew that Cindy's child lived, and like all the other skeletons in his closet, he made no point to hover about the grave. He hadn't even made an effort to keep tabs on her. To him, she was as dead as if she'd been snuffed out that afternoon on a cold, hard counter.

Oh, but the volcano of fury that boiled beneath the surface of his cold, calculating demeanor. He'd wondered how a poor college student could afford to retain the prestigious Finch, Walters & Associates to represent her in a simple adoption case. Who knew that Janice was Rachel's mother?

The senator recalled the thought that, with Janice Finch mucking about in the affair, bulldog that she was, the whole mess would blow wide open and cost him the election, and the millions of state dollars with it. Unwilling to risk that, the closed adoption seemed to be his only option. How he wished he had just done away with the brat when he'd had the chance. Now, she could ruin everything he'd worked for.

Cindy, however . . .

To say Cindy was surprised was like calling Niagara Falls a small leak.

Cindy's face was ashen. Like Mercy, she held a death grip on her chair—but hers wasn't out of grief. It was out of panic. Her entire universe had dissolved around her, sucking her down like quicksand. The stars were dust above her, stealing her breath and clouding her vision. The earth was water, stormy, and uncertain—threatening to drag her at any moment deep into the abyss.

Each eternal heartbeat rang in her ears like great gongs, beating out her doom. Her chest tightened with a vicelike grip. Air refused to fill her aching lungs. Prickly stars danced before her eyes, drawing ever tighter circles in her vision.

Lies! All lies! Everything she'd known was a lie.

Her baby was alive. Her father knew. He had to. The arguments she made that abortion was good and right, that she'd made the right choice, that she'd helped thousands of other girls make the right choice—all crumbled like a house of cards and lay scattered, cluttering the stage like autumn leaves.

She didn't *think* these thoughts … exactly. She simply *knew* them. She'd *always* known them. She'd just been working so hard to salve her guilt, to fill her sense of loss, and to punish herself for her choice, that she'd never been willing to face those truths.

Now the world no longer revolved around the sun, the sky was not blue, ice was not cold, water was not wet, the moon wasn't up, nor the earth down. Her world had been shaken so deeply that she no longer knew what was true.

The spinning universe overwhelmed her. She was falling.

Falling.

Forever falling.

Another heartbeat. Her vision cleared for a moment. Rene and Rachel knelt over her. Their mouths moved silently. Then like a slow, ponderous subway car, their voices trundled toward her, cutting through the fog. Yet they seemed distant, as if they were calling to her from the mouth of a deep cavern.

"Cindy! Are you OK? Are you all right?? Someone call 911!"

Cindy's vision clouded again.

Another heartbeat. It rang deafeningly in her ears. She didn't know how long she'd been there. She still felt like she was falling.

Her vision cleared again for a moment. Now, paramedics knelt over her. They moved in high gear, giving her an oxygen mask, checking her pulse, and asking her questions, but she felt like she was watching a silent movie. She could hear nothing. She could feel nothing.

Nothing but the heartbeat.

Her vision clouded again, and time disappeared.

Falling.

Always falling.

Nothing felt firm. Nothing was clear. Only the deep, slow, incessant pounding of the huge drum—the drum that spelled her doom.

Paramedics pressed through the throng, wheeling the immobilized Cindy into the ambulance. Cast, crew, crowd—and the simply curious—watched a youngish woman, strapped to a gurney like a mental patient, get loaded onto the awaiting "meat wagon." Paramedics clambered in after her and the vehicle sped away, lights flashing.

Rachel and Mercy stood watching from a distance. Mercy was still shaking and lightheaded from her monumental emotional shock.

"I'm sorry, honey. I had no idea," Rachel consoled, holding her tightly.

"She *hates* me, Mom," Mercy whispered in agony.

"She doesn't *know* you, honey. She might feel very different if she knew what I know."

Almost as if subconsciously refusing to let someone else supplant Rachel's place as her mother, Mercy rested her tearful head on Rachel's shoulder.

"You are the very best thing that ever happened to me. I do not regret even one moment with you."

Mercy nodded and the two fell silent, both eternally grateful for the company of the other.

Near the now-empty spot where the ambulance had parked, Catherine and Rene stood together. A top studio executive was just walking away, fury painted across his face. An intense conversation had just ended, and Catherine tried to encourage Rene.

"No, no, no. I think you're OK."

"All I know," Rene replied, shaken, "is I won't ever do an episode like *that* again."

Catherine nodded in agreement. It had been a red-letter day. The network was already fielding complaints from dozens of advertisers.

"Why don't we give everyone a week off?" Catherine suggested.

"That's fine with me," Rene agreed.

The studio executive charged through the crowd toward Parker, who was observing the scene from a more secluded corner of the back lot. Parker leaned against the wall, smoking and pondering the mass of revelations and surprises of the day. The biggest surprise, in his mind, was how utterly nonplussed his friend Senator Stevens had been about the entire drama. He was a politician, certainly, but even politicians have their weak points, right?

Senator Stevens, flanked as usual by his henchman, stepped from a nearby door and paused by Parker for a moment.

"That went well," Stevens noted sarcastically, crossing his arms.

Parker glanced over, gauging his friend's expression. He blew a cloud of smoke and knocked the ashes from the stick, his gaze turning back to the milling crowd.

"You already knew, didn't you?"

"I should have done something about that brat the day she was born," Stevens retorted coldly.

Parker was incredulous at the senator's callous nonchalance. "Your own granddaughter!?"

Stevens shot a murderous glance toward Parker, and the conversation paused as both pondered the future of their friendship.

"I'm very disappointed," the senator responded at last.

Parker opened his mouth to reply but was interrupted by the executive. With a gesture, the top brass ordered him to follow. Parker snuffed out his smoke and tossed the butt to the ground. With resignation, he swung his massive limbs into motion and followed. As he stepped away, he shot back a final parting comment. "Don't expect me to clean up your messes!"

Then the senator stood alone, smarting from the failures of the day.

CHAPTER TWELVE

Conversations

The cue light on Camera One flashed rapidly. Rene took a deep breath, mentally preparing for the show to go live.

Rene sported fall colors, featuring a deep rust-colored sweater dress girded with a glittery gold belt. Midnight-purple leggings, tipped with rust-red heels, completed the outfit. A matching gold necklace and bracelet glittered in the brilliant stage lights.

Everything was different. Parker, for one, was nowhere to be seen. The set was different as well—*completely* different. Instead of one broad stage with overstuffed seats (too "man cave," in Rene's opinion), it had been divided into three sections. Center stage featured a comfortably feminine seating area with the feel of a living room. Elegant seats surrounding an exquisite coffee table invited guests to relax and sip their coffee over warm conversation. Stage left was wide open, bordered by midnight blue curtains "glittered" with lit stars, and might, in any episode, feature a band, comedian, author, or even a dancing bear. It could be decked out to look like a den, a Christmas tree farm, a stage, a garden—anything Rene could imagine. In this episode, it was dressed like a little English garden with risers and would, later in the show, be featuring the Vienna Boys Choir.

Stage right, where audience attention was now focused, was modeled like a high-end home kitchen. Copper-plated stainless pots and pans hung from a ceiling rack. An obsidian colored cook top, centering the cooking island, shone like a midnight mirror. Beneath it, a glass-backed oven allowed guest chefs to tantalize audiences with yet-to-be-served dishes. The heavy bamboo cutting station, conveniently located to the right of the cook top, covered a stylish cherry cabinet suite. To the left, a glittering black marble countertop invited guests to gather and feast. Leather-upholstered cherrywood barstools lined the island, promising luxurious comfort to guests chosen to enjoy the delectable samples. Behind the chef, glass cabinet doors showcased a neatly arranged array of exquisite china.

Rene leaned casually against the island. Mouthwatering scents wafted from the stage oven, causing many a stomach in the audience to growl with hunger. She bantered jovially with the chef, "Jaques Petit," whom she knew quite well. In fact, this character was none other than Ralph, the resident odd duck, who was completing one of the popular character skits that made Rene's show famous.

Even the name had changed. With Parker gone, it became *Conversations with Rene*, and Rene was in charge. She brought to this show the same aplomb and style that had lifted *Parker & Rene* from obscurity. Touted by critics as the next Oprah, Rene had advanced from being a mere host to becoming a household brand. She, the young woman with the big heart, powerful personality, and wickedly savvy business sense, had become the go-to celebrity for nearly anyone hoping for wealth and fame.

As the audience awaited the segment to go live, a Pampers commercial played over the monitors. The end card leapt onto the screen as the cue light of Camera One lit up a solid, brilliant red. The monitor faded to black, the music swelled, then Rene appeared, larger than life, on the studio monitors. With a cue from the stage director, she greeted the audience.

"Welcome back! Now, let's see what has happened with the Atlantic salmon that our chef, Jaques Petit, has been preparing. I can't wait to sink my fork into this."

There was an ironic, almost comically sarcastic, tone in her comment, and the audience giggled in response.

Ralph's skits were always funny and surprising, often featuring a bit of magic. He'd play the oddest characters from the world over, entertain with put-on accents, fill the stage with antics, and leave the audience in stitches. In each skit, Ralph would purport to teach something, run into "unexpected" obstacles, find wacky solutions, then "magically" end the segment in some brilliantly entertaining way.

Today, Ralph, playing Chef Jaques Petit, was teaching the proper preparation of salmon for a special event. Only, his salmon was missing, so he used frozen fish sticks. The lemon was spoiled; the pepper was stuck and clumpy. His various garnishes were dry or unavailable. His choices for replacements left the audience moaning in disgust or laughing hilariously. Once in the oven, the audience could see the dish and see it wasn't tampered with.

Jaques, sporting a fake mustache, an unusually tall chef's hat, white double-buttoned kitchen smock, and gloved with oven mitts, pulled the dish from the oven, setting it on the island. Instead of the hodgepodge disaster the audience expected, a perfectly bronze, beautifully seasoned, spectacularly garnished salmon bake sizzled in the pan. The audience gasped in delight. Rene was no less pleased.

"May I?" She poised her fork in anticipation.

"Bon a-Petit," Jaques replied, with a deep, fake French accent.

He lifted his fork to join her, and each broke off a sumptuous morsel of fish. The bite melted in Rene's mouth. She could hardly believe her taste buds. Ralph never pulled the same gag twice, and this one topped everything he'd done so far.

"Mmmm! Ralph—excuse me, Jaques! You have really outdone yourself this time. This is unbelievable!"

"Merci, madame."

The audience tittered jovially at his act.

"How in the world did you do this!? I saw you put it in the oven. I saw it with my own eyes!"

Maintaining his accent, Jaques gave a broad flourish of his hand. "Zee magician never give up his secret." Jaques bowed as the audience laughed and applauded warmly.

Rene smiled broadly, shaking her head at his fun and surprising antics. She joined in the applause. "Thank you, Jaques."

Ralph bowed deeply and exited the stage, muttering every French word he knew—or thought he knew—and waving broadly. "Bienvenu! Merci beau coup, and now adieu to you, and you, and you!"

The audience rose in ovation, laughing, clapping, whistling, and cheering. Ralph exited the stage and disappeared as Rene made her way back to center stage. Camera Two rolled forward to tighten in on the shot as she introduced the show's next segment. The applause died away, and the crowd regained their seats.

"Now, our next guest today is, despite her young age, a veteran of our show. A published author at only sixteen, her book, *An Angel's Blood*, rocketed to the top of the Amazon nonfiction charts, where it remained for an astounding *seven weeks*. A surprise hit, though no surprise to me, women everywhere have found hope and healing in her words. We welcome Mercy Patterson.

"Also joining us is her mother, a registered nurse and medical instructor. A woman of uncommon love, courage, and good sense, please help me welcome Rachel Patterson."

Warm, welcoming applause filed the studio as Rachel and Mercy took the stage, waving happily. Rene gave each a friendly hug, then they sat down to fresh hot mugs of coffee. The tone of their reunion was quite different from how it had been more than a year ago. The uncertainty was gone, and the three met as if they were old friends joining for Sunday tea.

Rachel's Sisjuly ensemble was, again, reminiscent of the fifties. All black with a white belt and accents, the tea-length polyester dress featured a sleeveless bodice with raindrop cutouts along the broad scoop-neck collar. Peeking beneath her full skirt, she sported red patent-leather heels that practically glowed in the stage lights, and black nylon stockings knit in a checkerboard pattern. Her long auburn hair was tied up in an inverted braid that almost looked like a hairnet, and it was topped off with a cherry-red hair bow.

Mercy, looking a bit more grown-up, featured a red satin blouse with pleated front and a black pencil skirt. The short sleeves on the blouse cuffed and buttoned, giving it a hint of French style. The buttons were plated a sort of red gold, giving the impression that the blouse had been tastefully bedazzled. Her long blond hair was tied back neatly—almost professionally—with a thin black ribbon. She wore red suede pumps that matched her blouse and, as always, her left arm showcased a long black lace glove, girded about with her ever-present red pro-life bracelet.

"Mercy, welcome back," Rene offered, opening the conversation.

"Thanks for having me, Miss Weeks."

Rene waved the formality away. "Please, 'Rene' is fine."

She turned to Rachel, welcoming her as well.

"My pleasure," Rachel responded warmly.

"Mercy, how have you been since you were here last?"

"Wow! It's been a roller-coaster ride. The book went further than I ever imagined, and people now come up to me in the grocery store or at restaurants and tell me their stories. I'm really blown away by the impact my book has had.

"I just thought people needed to know Bridget's story. I had no idea so many people had such deep wounds of their own."

"I'm so glad you wrote it, Mercy," Rene replied. "As you know, it was very eye opening for me. It really forced me to rethink a lot of things I assumed that I knew. Thank you so much for your courage in putting the story out there.

"What is the best thing you've experienced since writing the book?"

Mercy pondered how to convey the rich experiences she had enjoyed.

"I think the very best thing I've experienced is meeting the girls who've taken a different path than they had considered. They chose to gift life to their children. Sometimes I even get to meet those babies. It's a real blessing. A few of the girls have been named Mercy, after me. I can't express how honored I am to have been a part of their lives. Of saving a life—or maybe two."

"Yes," Rene agreed, "it is good to help other girls avoid the tragedy Bridget suffered."

"And the girls I talk with thank me over and over, because they never realized—amid all of the talk about a ruined life, college, and careers—that children are a priceless blessing."

"That's certainly been my experience," Rachel added. "I could never have known in advance the beautiful treasure that Mercy would be. It would have been a quick, 'easy' decision for me to just—well—'end her' right there on the table. Instead, I rescued her, and that was the most beautiful decision I ever made."

"And the crazy thing is," Rene pointed out, "that Mercy wasn't even your child at that point. She wasn't your responsibility, and she wouldn't have had any impact on your life, one way or the other, before that moment. Yet you chose to save her, eventually becoming her mother. All of those—shall we say—'risks' other single moms assume by keeping their babies, you took those on willingly."

Rachel nodded.

"At any point," Rene continued, "you could have jumped ship. You could have done your job. You could have left her in the hospital or put her into foster care. You could have done just about anything, and probably no one would have thought worse of you, but you kept her. You put your future at risk. That's just mind blowing. Why did you do it?"

By this point, Rachel's eyes had filled with tears, and her voice grew husky. "At first it was because I knew it was right. I saved her because it was right. Through college, I fought to defend women from exploitation by the patriarchy, and in that moment, I realized that here was a woman who was being abused by a practice I thought was *defending* women. I realized that this industry was the most horrid sort of patriarchal exploitation on the planet, and I just couldn't stand for it anymore.

"And then I—"

Rachel couldn't go on. The tears flowed uncontrollably. Mercy squeezed her hand affectionately. After a few moments, she was able to continue.

"Then I fell in love with her and couldn't imagine life without her. I'd trade everything all over again to be her mother. And really, there was no trade," Rachel added, dabbing her eyes dry. "All of the most beautiful blessings I have enjoyed have come because of her."

Mercy laid her head on her mom's shoulder, her heart swelling with gratefulness at her mother's sacrifices.

"My goodness," Rene exclaimed, "she certainly *is* a treasure. And a fighter too. I mean, with all of the experiences she's had, to have survived them. It's just remarkable!"

"Providential," Mercy replied.

Rachel and Rene nodded in agreement.

"What would you say," Rene continued, turning her focus back to Mercy, "was the hardest thing you've encountered since writing the book?"

"Well—you may not believe this . . . I certainly didn't—but I have perfect strangers coming up to me and saying things like, 'You should have died that day and saved the world from your bigotry' or 'You're such a brat! You have no right to speak out against women's rights like that.' Some people are so rude.

"It kind of hurts, because, I mean, how do they know who I am? What right do they have to say I shouldn't be alive, just because they disagree with what I say? I mean, those are the kinds of people that would kill a baby that's lying on a counter simply because she's supposed to have died, right?"

"Wow! That's harsh. So how have you dealt with those kinds of comments?"

"Well, if they're on Amazon, I just don't read them. Haters will be haters. But when they do it in person, Mom and I talk through it. It doesn't happen very often.

"When Mom is with me though, boy! You should see 'momma bear' come out! She takes them on!"

The audience laughed with her at the thought of Rachel, gentle and kind, going nuclear on someone who had accosted her daughter.

"I do!" Rachel added, almost defensively. "I really do."

"I can only imagine," Rene added. "In fact, we got a little taste of that during the last show. Cindy Pierce, if you remember, made some similar comments during the show."

"Oh, I remember," Rachel affirmed.

"Mercy, how did you feel, hearing that from Cindy?"

Mercy's eyes welled with tears. She choked up, unable to reply.

"She was crushed," Rachel answered for her.

"Not long after that," Rene continued, "you learned that Cindy Pierce was your birth mother. What did you feel when you learned that?"

"I couldn't really describe how I felt. Shock—really. It just didn't seem real."

"When did it sink in that it was true?"

"Mom had already told me the story—some of it is even in my book. But I never imagined I would actually meet her."

"Many of the emotions and fears Mercy had as a child," Rachel added, "came swarming back. It was a very difficult time for her."

Mercy's face still flushed from the emotion of that first meeting with Cindy.

Rene was sympathetic and gentle. "I can see that even now," Rene offered in a hushed tone, "this is still a painful spot for you. Can you tell me what some of those emotions and fears were?"

"I just—" Mercy answered with difficulty. "I imagined what my life might have been like if she had kept me. I wondered . . . I wondered why she didn't want me . . . why she couldn't stand the thought of keeping me."

Rachel squeezed her hand consolingly.

"The things she said—" Mercy began, choking with uncontrollable tears.

After a few moments, she regained her composure and continued. "I know she hates me."

It was clear to Rene and the audience that the wound still ran deep. The pain of being unwanted cut like a hot knife, despite the span of time she had faced and ocean of love she had received since that horrific moment.

Camera Two was close in on Mercy, broadcasting each steaming tear in living detail. Monitors throughout the studio played the very real, painful drama for everyone to see.

Rene gave Mercy a few moments of peace as she grieved the loss she had suffered. Three cups of coffee rested, cold and forgotten, on the table in front of them. Though few audience members had seen the original interview, many eyes were moist in sympathy for the brave but brokenhearted young woman.

As Rachel and Mercy dried their tears with their own tissues, Rene continued. "So how do you deal with such an earth-shattering revelation?"

Mercy and Rachel paused for a few moments. They glanced at each other questioningly, as mothers and daughters do when they've shared significant experiences. Mercy tried to formulate the words to answer, but they wouldn't come.

Seeing her difficulty, Rachel interjected. "It has been a very long road. Very hard."

Rene leaned in closely, as a friend entering into a secret confidence. Her eyes were gentle and her voice soft. She had a question that could be as hurtful as healing, and wanted to make certain, if there was any way possible, to make this moment—this question—a step toward healing. "Mercy, if there were anything you could have from Cindy, what would it be?"

Mercy thought for a moment, her face still red from the heat of emotion. Finally, she glanced up. Her face was open, like a book that could be read by all. Her voice was soft as a whisper. "I would want her to want me."

Rene let the wish hang in the air.

The studio was still. One could almost hear the roaring thunder of a tiny pin clattering against the concrete floor. Rene glanced away, reaching quietly for her cup and saucer, lifting them nearly to her chin. She took a long, silent sip. The saucer tinkled lightly as she replaced the cup on it. Her motion was smooth—almost automatic—as if she were lost in thought.

Mercy, too, seemed lost in an alternate universe. Thoughts of what might have been spun through her young mind. She knew that the idyllic world of her fantasy could never have played out in real life. No one on earth could have been a better mother to her than the woman sitting next to her on the couch. She was certain of that. Yet nothing could prevent her girlish imagination from conjuring scenes of snuggling, reading, playing, and dancing with her "real" mom—the lost years. Now that she had a face to paint over the name "mother," she felt as if she watched sorrowfully through a mirror as some little girl, who looked much like she did (but without the scars), enjoyed the beauty of life with her mother.

Rachel pondered the moment as well. Torn by the agony her daughter felt and the guilt of her own failings as a mom, she, too, took her silent sip of the tepid coffee. She'd done the best she could and had even been up front with Mercy about how everything came to be. Yet in that moment, she was still unable to prevent the crushed heart her beloved daughter experienced when she actually faced her birth mother for the first time. No one can describe the pain a mother feels when her child is hurting. No one can understand a mother's agony. No one but another mother.

After a long, seemingly eternal, pause, Rene recaptured the moment. The wish still hanging in the air, Rene had a question. "Do you feel that is possible?"

"I don't know," Mercy replied simply.

Though the conversation was really getting to the heart of Mercy's experience, Rene didn't want to stray too far from the topic of the show. Deftly, she brought Mercy's book back into the conversation.

"Mercy, your book takes a very candid look at these questions and your struggle for healing, doesn't it?"

Mercy nodded.

"Have you found closure in this situation?"

"I'm getting there. I've been learning how to forgive."

"That seems like a lot to forgive."

"It is, but I have a good example. Even while He was still hanging on the cross, Jesus said, 'Father, forgive them, because they do not know what they are doing.'"

Rene took another long sip of her coffee. She seemed confused—even a little surprised. The coffee gave her a moment to formulate a response that didn't sound unprofessional. The miraculous properties of the coffee—or perhaps time and good sense—gave her the answer. "That's very noble. I'm not sure I could do that."

"I can't forgive like that either, but I know He can give me the power to."

"So, you aren't angry? You don't think she might deserve some retribution or something?"

"I've been angry at points—and very hurt. The fact is, we all deserve some retribution, so I have no right to hold Cindy's wrongs against her while expecting God to let my wrongs slide."

"What wrongs could you possibly have done at your age?" Rene asked incredulously.

"If you only knew," Mercy teasingly responded.

"She wrote a little about *that* in her book too," Rachel inserted, smiling.

With a bit of an "Oh really?" expression, Rene faced the audience. "Another reason to get Mercy's book."

Everyone chuckled good naturedly at the pleasant jibe.

"So," Rene continued, "as a child, you were dealing with the pain of rejection. You got all of those emotions behind you—then you were suddenly looking into your birth mother's face. Did you find forgiveness to be easy in that moment?"

Mercy looked away, emotions swirling like a tornado inside her. Too many thoughts sprang to mind. She couldn't answer. The silence grew uneasy. Still, words would not come.

Rachel watched the storm flash across her daughter's face and squeezed her hand. "Her wounds are still pretty raw."

Rene reached over and squeezed Mercy's hand as well. It was clear that Mercy was more than a guest to Rene. She was a friend. Their connection, which had begun during that first episode, had grown into a kindred-spirit friendship—two young women who were strong and courageous, each sharing a respect and admiration for the other. Rene truly wanted Mercy's remarkable message to impact millions, and she was wholly unwilling to exploit Mercy's pain for show ratings. That said, ratings would help Mercy's cause. Even more, what Rene had planned might help Mercy heal.

"Mercy, do you recall, when we booked this show a few weeks ago, I mentioned that Cindy has something to tell you. Are you ready to hear it?"

Mercy glanced toward her mother, tears still dancing in her lashes, then took a deep, ragged breath. "I would like to say I am, but . . ." She was unable to articulate her thoughts any farther.

"I will not press you," Rene asserted, "but I think you will want to hear what she has to say."

Mercy was reticent. Still smarting from the harsh words cast at her more than a year ago, she felt like a puppy cowering in a corner as mean boys cast painful rocks. She didn't know if she dared risk more pain, more rejection. But she trusted Rene. Rene had always had her back, even when they disagreed. Now, Rene was a full-fledged proponent of Life. If Rene felt it would be a good thing, Mercy felt she could dare.

"OK," Mercy reluctantly agreed.

Rene turned toward the audience.

"Let's take a break. When we come back, we'll hear a special message from Mercy's birth mother."

The brilliant white screen faded into a slow-motion close-up of two young children clambering from their car and dashing into their grandmother's arms. Their father held the door open, watching them proudly as they expressed their irrepressible delight.

Gentle music swelled as a compassionate, motherly voice commented. "I could never imagine life without them."

Just as the children threw their arms around her, the image paused, holding for a heartbeat. Suddenly, the motion reversed. The laughing children dashed backward—time whizzing its way into the past.

The image stopped for a moment, revealing a wedding. The grandmother tearfully watched her son get married, the dashing young man glowing as he looked into his gorgeous bride's eyes.

"You may now kiss the bride," the minister's echoing, distant voice pronounced.

He bent to press his lips to hers.

The image froze again, then reversed full speed and flew away to another memory of the distant past. The blindingly fast rewind settled on a crowd walking backward into a gymnasium. Everyone regained their seats, and the graduates marched backward across the stage until one young man reached the steps leading up to the platform.

Again, the image paused, giving everyone a moment to see that this was the same man, though younger, who had just married the girl.

"Nicky Vance, *cum laude*."

His name called, he marched proudly across the stage to accept his diploma. His mother watched his victory with teary-eyed delight, applauding energetically as he made his wave and bow.

Suddenly, the image reversed again. In a moment, the stage was gone, and a little league baseball field took its place. Players ran around the bases backward until one lad got up to bat.

Pausing again, before it replayed the moment, the image held on a young determined face. It was the same fellow who had graduated from high school. Now he was barely twelve and up to plate. The pitcher threw a low ball.

From the stands, his mother shouted, "You can do it!!"

The ball flew toward him in slow motion. His powerful swing arched across the base, racing toward the rocketing curve ball. As the bat and ball crossed paths, the bat grabbed nothing but air. A loud *crack* resounded as the ball landed safely in the catcher's mitt. The bat swung wildly, and the youth's expression, in that agonizingly slow shot, showed that he knew the jig was up.

"You're out!!" the umpire cried.

Dejectedly, he schlumped to the dugout, threw his bat on the ground, flopped onto the bench, and buried his face in his hands. His now-concerned mother craned her neck to see how her disappointed boy fared in the dugout. She clearly hurt with him.

Again, the scene reversed rapidly, racing back to events of the boy's history. The frantic rewinding stopped to reveal the boy, barely four years old, playing in a park gym. His mother, now much younger, sat on a nearby bench, conversing cordially with another young mother. The lad, taking an unusually bold dare, slipped, fell to the ground, and skinned his knee. Hearing his cry, his mother dashed over, examined his wound and soothed away his pain.

Time again flew. Zooming back to a quiet moment in a dimly lit apartment, the image again paused. Mom was reading by lamplight. She reclined in a rocking chair so the infant snoozing on her breast could rest comfortably. He squirmed a little, restless, drawing her attention away from the book. She put it down and began to sing, patting him gently. The little bit calmed down and returned to his soft rhythmic breathing.

Time raced backward one last time.

A young couple were fighting. The same woman, now noticeably pregnant, listened stunned and teary eyed as her boyfriend lambasted her.

"How could you do this?" he screamed. "You were supposed to be *careful*. You were supposed to be using precautions!"

"Well, if you weren't so pushy," she retorted bitterly, "it might have worked!"

"Look. I didn't sign on for this. You're not going to trap me with this baby crap. You take care of the problem or we're through."

"Joey, please," she pleaded.

He just pushed her away and stormed out of the dorm room. She threw herself onto the bed, melting into irrepressible sobs.

A kind voice spoke over the heartbreaking image.

"Pregnant and alone? When the world couldn't be darker, we can give you light. We've been where you are, and we're here to help. Call now and find your hope for a brighter future."

The screen faded to white, and a logo appeared—New Life Crisis Center—with a toll-free phone number. The image held on as the inviting music played to its end, then the screen faded to black.

This was the local feed rebroadcast in the studio, allowing Catherine to confirm the quality of the feed. Everyone in the switcher room had their eyes glued to the monitors. While the local ad played on the tuner monitor, the broadcast-out monitor showed the countdown for the local ad slots. Other monitors showed the various cameras fixed on their zero stations—their starting positions for the beginning of the next segment.

The director had Camera Two framed on a close-up of Rene, Camera One framed on the logo, Camera Three featuring everyone already on the stage, and Camera Four aimed with anticipation of where a new guest would emerge onto the stage. Rene and the logo were punched up on the preview monitors, and everyone was ready. The slug had counted to three when the commercial ended. A two-second beat—almost a bated breath— and the music swelled.

"Go One," the director ordered.

The broadcast monitor lit up with the logo. The operator zoomed out quickly to reveal the full stage and panned across the guests.

"Go Two," the director ordered, and the image switched to the close-up of Rene.

"Welcome back to *Conversations*," Rene began. "Before the break, we heard Mercy's story of meeting her birth mother. Now, Mercy has agreed to hear a special message from her birth mother, Cindy Pierce. Once the director of New Dawn Women's Clinics, Cindy has taken a very different direction in life over the last year. We will hear her story now."

Rene looked to Mercy compassionately, took her hand, and asked gently, "Mercy, are you ready?"

Mercy looked down and nodded tentatively as a medley of mixed emotions tore across her heart.

Still gently holding Mercy's hand, Rene turned to the audience. "Please help me welcome Cindy Pierce."

Applause filed the studio as Cindy stepped from behind a curtain and onto the stage. Gone was the hardness and arrogance. The face was the same, but hardly much else. Her subdued manner seemed more authentic than her previous grinning confidence. Her therapist, Karen, slipped from a side door and took a visible seat in the front row. Cindy glanced her way as uncertainly washed over her, and Karen gave her a quick smile of encouragement.

Cindy settled near Rene, opposite to Rachel and Mercy. Rather than her typical power-suit attire, she looked more "soccer mom" in appearance. She had grown out her hair and wore it down. Her new style softened her middle-aged features, lending an air of rejuvenated youth. A pastel-pink blouse complemented her stone-colored slacks, and burgundy flats promised comfort rather than power. A sheer burgundy scarf completed the ensemble. Though she remained composed, heartstrings clearly resonated below the surface, threatening to burst forth at any moment.

"Welcome, Cindy," Rene offered.

"Thank you for having me," Cindy responded.

"How have you been?"

"Better," Cindy replied quietly. "It was very painful for a while."

"You spent some time in recovery," Rene began, offering a moment for Cindy's response.

"Yes."

"And have been in therapy," Rene continued.

"Yes," came the simple response. Cindy glanced back to Karen, who just nodded encouragingly.

"What was it like to discover that your daughter was still alive?"

Tears welled up in Cindy's eyes, and she choked on the upswell of passion that swirled in her heart.

Rene reached out sympathetically, touching her arm gently.

Cindy took a deep breath. "It was like . . . like someone sucked all the air out of me."

"Why?"

Cindy struggled to condense a year of introspection into a single coherent thought. "I had built my whole life around the guilt I had for killing her—then suddenly the whole edifice was gone. I didn't know who I was or what was real."

"And you had a nervous breakdown?" Rene queried.

Cindy nodded. "I spent, I think," Cindy added, looking to Karen for confirmation, "six months at the Meadows and have been in therapy since then."

Rene was careful to be gentle, conversational, and affirming in her questions. Before the last episode, Cindy had, of course, been a guest a few times and was a favored connection of Parker's, but Cindy and Rene had never really connected. After the breakdown and as part of her recovery, Cindy wrote to Rene, apologizing for her conduct on the show. Rene came to respect her because of it, and a new friendship had been formed. She'd even begun to view Cindy as a big sister in need of family support and healing. They had agonized over this show but concluded— based on Karen's expertise—that this would be a key step in healing not just for Cindy, but for Mercy as well.

Rene continued her questions. "What has been the most helpful in your recovery?"

"Well," Cindy offered haltingly, "I read Mercy's book."

She glanced furtively toward the young woman to measure her reaction. Mercy was, understandably, shocked. So was the audience.

"You did?" Rene asked incredulously.

"Yes. I didn't . . . I don't . . . understand it all. It gave me hope, though, that I could . . . move on . . . find healing. What I read gave me the courage to get up each morning."

"What offered you the most hope?"

"Well, though she had never met me, she spoke of how her religion helped ease her anger toward me. I guess . . . I don't know how religion could do that . . . but I wanted to know more."

Rene was intrigued. This wasn't a direction she had anticipated.

"Mercy," Rene asked, "how has your religion impacted your ability to put your hurt behind you?"

"It's not religion," Mercy replied earnestly. "Religion is just a bunch of rules. I have a *relationship* with God—a friendship with the creator of the universe. He showed me what love really was—and that He loved me passionately. He showed me all the remarkable miracles He had done in my life to get me here."

To Cindy, all of that seemed like a foreign language. People spoke of God like he was their dad. That was a view she simply couldn't get her mind around. Every time she thought, "Father," one image leaped to her mind—*her* father. And he wasn't a great guy. Certainly not someone she could trust or rely on. Most definitely not someone who worked to have a close relationship with her. He was harsh, overbearing and impossible to please. Try as she might, she couldn't imagine God as any different.

"But how," Cindy wondered, "can you be . . . like . . . *friends* with God? How can you know there even *is* a God?"

"Those are some big questions," Rene added.

Mercy nodded.

"They are," Rachel responded, "and you know, Cindy, they don't have any easy answers. Simple, yes, but to answer them, we must dig deeply into what is true."

"I just started with Jesus—who He is," Mercy offered, "what He claimed. If He is exactly what He claimed to be, He is alive right now and has the power to heal me."

"I really wish I could believe all that."

"Cindy," Rachel wondered, "when the show wraps, would you be open to getting some coffee? We could talk more."

"I don't want to impose."

"It would be no imposition at all." Rachel smiled.

Noticing the time, Rene redirected the conversation to the actual reason Cindy had come on the show. "Cindy, you have written a letter for Mercy, haven't you?"

Cindy nodded, the passion welling up again.

"Would you like to read that for us?" Rene asked.

"Yes." Cindy pulled the letter from her pocket, unfolded it, and began to read. The page was worn, torn and soiled by dirt and tears. It was obvious the words were treasured and often read.

"Dear Mercy,

"I know you may never read this, but even if not, I want to tell you how sorry I am—how much I truly regret not getting to be your mother. No one ever told me the guilt and heartache I would feel at losing you. They always said it was painless, easy. I told many women the same thing.

"I *didn't* tell them that the day you died, so did I. I felt you move when I was pregnant, and all of a sudden, I felt nothing. My mind and my heart went numb, and I felt like a piece of me—of who I was—was gone forever.

"I died the moment they took you away and I never got to hold you in my arms.

"I missed your first smile, your first steps, your first day of school, your first tooth falling out. One decision truly can change the rest of your life—and I made the wrong one.

"Being dead makes a person cold and hard, even cruel. I had nothing real to live for. I let my pain and guilt quench every spark of life in my soul.

"Then one day I discovered you were not dead, and it reignited the spark. I had been numb so long, I didn't even know what living was like, but I knew I could finally live.

"Now, I am thrilled to see what a beautiful, intelligent, capable woman you have become, and it breaks my heart that I could not be a part of your life.

"I totally understand if you hate me and never want to see me again. I know that is how I would feel if I were in your position. I know I do not deserve to be forgiven—not only for what I did to you but for what I have done to so many others.

"You talk in your book of a God who forgives. I do not know if there is a God, and I can't really imagine being forgiven for what I've done. But if I could have your forgiveness, I could hope—at least—that it's possible.

"I am so thankful for your mother's kind heart and her love for you. You have been raised to be such a wonderful person. Please continue your fight to save these babies and their mothers from the heartache of abortion. Don't give up! I am so very proud of you. I wish with all my heart that I could call you my daughter."

Quietly, without another word, Cindy folded the much-read letter and clasped it in her hands. Not an eye in the building was dry. Here and there throughout the room were heard the quiet sobs of women who knew all too well the pain Cindy had suffered.

Then a clap rang out. And another. A wave of emotion lifted the audience to its feet in thunderous, supportive applause.

When finally the clapping died down, Rene had dried her tears and found her voice. "Cindy, that was very beautiful."

Too emotional to respond, Cindy said nothing.

A long, momentous pause hung in the studio air. No one knew just how to continue.

A particularly shuddering sob was cut short. A woman, sitting near the front row, fought against the ocean of regret that overwhelmed her. She might have been fifty years old but had a youthfulness that shielded her true age. She was sharply dressed and seemed like a well-educated, professional woman. She could easily have belonged in the C-suite of any major corporation. Her light locks framed her pleasantly plump cheeks, which were just beginning to spider with the wrinkles of a stressful work life. She seemed like one who, though smiling occasionally, found herself in the throes of weighty decisions.

Uncharacteristically, her eyes were reddened with tears.

She rose, casting a heartbreaking question toward the stage, hoping desperately that someone would help her find peace of mind.

"What do you do if you *know* your child didn't survive—"

CHAPTER THIRTEEN

Heart-to-Heart

The enticing scents of coffee and chocolate wafted through the lounge. Stirring spoons clinked and tinked as they formed whirlpools of foam in piping hot mugs of cappuccinos, espressos, Frappuccinos, and other exotically named hot beverages. All sorts of goodies dotted the tables with coffee essence and chocolate richness.

Coffections was the perfect place to meet for a chat over drinks. Though busy, the bright, homey café offered many cozy corners in which to chat. When a conversation would run long, one need but ask and a friendly server would bring such delights as Café Brulée, a crème brûlée with the bold notes of dark-roast Columbian, or perhaps a Café di Mezzanotte cheesecake, a slice of rich, creamy coffee cheesecake with an Oreo-cookie crust, shaved midnight chocolate on top, and an Italian dark-roast coffee syrup drizzle. Sometimes guests made their conversations drag on simply so they could justify another treat.

Rachel, Mercy, Cindy, and Karen found themselves in a private corner of this very establishment. Cindy had, after the show, taken Rachel up on her offer, and not wanting to overstep her bounds, had invited Karen to come moderate the discussion.

The four of them, cups in hand, had waded through the awkward greetings, the crowd of *Coffections* fans, and had landed on a quiet spot where they could hold their conversation in peace. Almost completely walled in, the space had comfortable leather-covered stuffed chairs arranged around a low round Asian-style table. An arch spanned the one opening to the outside world (the remainder of the restaurant), and a natural vine adorned it with the fresh green scent of life. A low fire in a small gas stove offered the comfortable feeling of warmth, while a large flat-screen TV hanging over top silently broadcast election coverage the ladies conspicuously ignored. Just outside the archway, an eternal water fountain whispered a soothing trickle, masking the conversation from passersby.

The coffee cooled comfortably as the four finished exchanging pleasantries. Almost like old friends, they'd filled in the gaps of time each had missed of the others' lives. It wasn't as if the past didn't matter—as if wrongs were forgotten—but that the new had grown over the old.

Life had supplanted death. Beauty was found in the fissures of devastation.

None had forgotten the prime purpose for their meeting, though no one knew how to turn the conversation toward the topic. Most of an hour had flown by when Rachel realized she must make that step.

"Cindy," Rachel began, "I know we are presuming on Dr. Karen's time, so I don't want to neglect your question too long."

"Oh, that's all right," Karen countered. "Take all the time you need. If it helps Cindy, I'm all for it."

"Thanks." Rachel smiled. "Cindy, you'd wondered how Mercy could forgive, right?"

"Yes," Cindy replied. "I just can't get my mind around this 'forgive and forget' thing. I mean, when someone has hurt me, I can't forget, no matter how hard I try. And trying makes me feel like I am excusing what they did or cheapening it in some way.

Sometimes, forgiving just doesn't even *feel* right. Do you know what I mean? So how can *Mercy* be able to forgive *me*?"

"I do know what you mean. And I really, really struggled with that myself. As you recall, I was an intern, so I'd assisted with several abortions that day before I got to Mercy. Once I realized what I had been a part of, I was just sick. It hit me all at once—that I could have known, but I didn't want to. And when I came face to face with the reality of what I was doing and defending, I was devastated. I couldn't understand how I'd let myself be tricked like that. After all, I was a strong-willed, independent woman.

"After that day, I could no longer even face myself in the mirror. My mom was supportive, but she didn't understand. She hadn't seen what I saw. For weeks I had nightmares about screaming, terrified children and axe murderers. It was horrible."

Cindy was startled by the revelation. "I had nightmares too. They started the moment I lost Mercy, and despite trying to drink it away, I had the same nightmare almost every night since then. So, do you still have the nightmares?"

"No, actually," Rachel replied, "those drifted away once I really came to understand forgiveness and how to accept it."

Rachel paused as she sipped her coffee for a moment while Cindy nodded encouragingly, intently listening for the key to the freedom that Rachel's story offered.

"Like you, I'd grown up believing that forgiveness is excusing people for what they did wrong and letting them get by with it. Forgiveness, to me, was what wimps did because they couldn't find a way to make the culprit pay.

"And my mother held a similar view. She was strong and liberated, just as was I, and she pretty much taught me that view. So, when I was so very obviously torn up about what I had done, she didn't know what do.

"A couple weeks later, a friend of mine in nursing school realized that I was sinking and took me aside. She was the religious goodie-two-shoes type, I thought, and would not be able to handle the situation without fainting or reaching for her rosary.

"But her response really shocked me. She didn't treat me as if I had Ebola or COVID. She was quiet for a good while. Then she plainly asked me if I wanted to be forgiven.

"For the life of me, I couldn't see how that related to anything. I had been tricked into complicity with the patriarchal abuse of women. I'd had the wool pulled over my eyes, and it was the fault of the WASP-controlled patriarchy that I was fooled and dragged into this. I was practically out for blood. I wanted men to pay for having deceived me.

"But she didn't buy any of that. She wasn't angry or accusatory. She didn't match my tone. She just calmly insisted on an answer— did *I* want to be forgiven? She kept asking me until I admitted frankly, to myself as much as to her, that I was wrong, and I knew it.

"It was like Niagara Falls crushing down on me. I was overwhelmed and suffocating. I knew I was wrong, and I knew that I had known the whole time. Forgiveness for me wasn't possible. Nothing could wash my slate clean. The blood stains would remain forever.

"But she kept insisting. She kept at it until it began to dawn on me—she actually *believed I* could be forgiven. But I still believed that forgiveness meant sweeping the issue under the rug, and I just couldn't buy into it.

"Then she told me a story I would never forget.

"A woman, every bit as wrong and vile as me, was caught in the very act of doing that evil thing. Arrested by the local authorities, she was unceremoniously hauled into a public square where the townspeople did their local business. It was common in those days for someone like that to be publicly executed on the spot for crimes such as she had committed—in fact, those punishments are still meted out today in that part of the world.

"It so happened that a famous teacher was there, and he was in the middle of one of his lessons. The authorities asked him his opinion of what should be done to her. They intended to bait him into losing favor with the public and so stop being a nuisance to the leaders.

"But the teacher simply ignored them. They pressed the question, and he still ignored them. After a few minutes of heat from these guys, and seeing the utter misery and despair of the woman they had arrested, this teacher began to write something in the dust.

"Still, the officials didn't give up. After hounding him some time for an answer, he looked up from the ground and said, 'Whoever is without sin in this matter may throw the first stone.' Then he bent back to the ground and continued to write.

"No one knows what he wrote, but he wrote and wrote and wrote. As his scribbles grew in the dust, officer after officer became shocked, then embarrassed. Each began to slink quietly away. Before long, the officials had all disappeared, leaving no one to hold or charge the woman.

"The teacher finally spoke, much to the curiosity of his followers, and asked a simple question, 'Woman, where are those who want to accuse you?'

"'They are all gone,' she replied.

"His next words shocked her. 'I do not condemn you either. Go your way, and do not do this anymore.'"

The story had captured Cindy's imagination, practically transporting her into that moment. As she painted the story in her mind, she didn't feel like a spectator. She felt as if she herself *was* the woman cowering in shame before the condemning eyes of the crowd, and her heart thrilled to the sound of the words, "I do not condemn you either."

"So," Rachel continued, "how could an ordinary man simply excuse the crime she'd committed? She had been caught in the act. Was he suggesting that her crime didn't matter?"

"What did she do wrong?" Cindy asked.

"That isn't really relevant at the moment, right? What matters is that what she did was as bad as what we did, and she was forgiven. But still, does that mean what she—what *we* did—was no big deal?"

"No," Cindy whispered, shame washing across her scarlet face.

Rachel looked at the broken woman with gentle eyes. "So how could this man offer her forgiveness—and be *right* to do so?"

Unable to speak, Cindy simply shook her head, shrugging slightly. A single tear crawled into the corner of her eye and tracked down her burning cheek.

"Because he was no ordinary man. What my friend told me that day changed my life. She told me that man was Jesus—*God Himself*—who came as a human, a real, flesh-and-blood human—whose entire goal on earth was to offer forgiveness to that woman, to me—to *you*. We deserve the most horrid punishments for what we did. We have all been truly monstrous.

"But rather than burying us forever under a mountain of stones, Jesus climbed a mountain, was lifted onto a cross, and died in our place. Our crimes *had* to be paid for. That was only right. But Jesus loved us so much he willingly took our place."

Cindy glanced up, meeting Rachel's gaze. Pain and hope washed silently across her eyes. She was clearly surprised. How could this be possible? If there even was a God, how could He know who she was, much less care about her? Yet here was Rachel, and her heart change was inexplicable—except for . . .

"This is where," Rachel continued, "forgiveness—*true* forgiveness—comes in. Real forgiveness is letting go of my right to judge and letting God be the judge—whether I'm judging myself or judging others. Real forgiveness is recognizing my own guilt and respecting the mercy God has already shown me by showing mercy to others, regardless of what they deserve.

"You see, I was so condemning of myself—and so blind to any way out—that I vehemently blamed others. I knew, deep in my heart, that what I had chosen to do was wrong, but I had justified it in my mind. I renamed it. I called it 'a woman's right to choose,' and I'd say, 'It's just a blob of tissue.' Deep inside I totally knew better—and then, when I was faced with the reality, I passed the blame. I accused men of deceiving me. I vowed to pay them back for tricking me. But I knew the whole time I had lied to myself.

"My friend showed me the way out of my darkness, and when I realized I could be free, I finally accepted the reality that I was the one who was wrong."

Cindy looked down thoughtfully, absently stirring her coffee, carefully weighing out everything Rachel had just said. The others leaned back in their seats to sip their drinks and ponder what they'd discussed. It had been a heavy conversation, and while they hadn't solved all the problems of the universe, they'd made a good start.

A waiter came by, and before long, each had another coffee on its way. Conversation turned to lighter topics, and laughter punctuated moments among tales and musings. Oblivious to the TV, the four didn't notice the latest election results pop up on the screen.

A cell phone rang.

A massive hand slid the gadget from its pocket and scanned the caller ID.

Stevens.

Parker scowled, rejected the call, and silenced the device.

Glancing toward the professional woman beside him, he apologized. "Sorry. Should have done that sooner."

She nodded acceptance. "We've got five minutes. Have a seat, and we'll get you wired up." She glanced down to her clipboard, then motioned Parker to his perch.

Parker nodded and stepped over to the news desk. He straightened his Kelly-green plaid suit as he slid his massive football-player frame into the chair. The other two anchors were already seated and being wired for sound.

"Ready?" Sam Flint asked him.

Sam was a veteran talking head. His ample silver locks swept back into a sharp, respectable hairdo. His charcoal suit and burgundy tie belied his conservative stance.

Parker nodded in response, tossing his signature smile back at Sam.

Claire Mendez, the moderator, flashed a momentary welcoming smile Parker's way, then got right back to business. "May I get a sound check?" she asked the frantic intern that fussed with her mic.

The intern nodded and signaled the sound man.

Sometimes a network will grab a drop-dead gorgeous model to stand in as eye candy for viewers—sports networks were notorious for this—but beautiful as she was, Claire was no eye candy. A feisty conservative, she had made a name for herself on YouTube, then was tapped to moderate the Clear Air Network's *Pan-America* show. Producers hoped to offer audiences a scintillating and balanced show that gave voice to both sides of hot issues, but they needed a strong, level-headed personality to keep it all on track. Claire was that guiding hand. Conversations on the program often grew heated, and Claire had a way of reining in arguments without crushing toes.

This was Parker's first episode as the liberal voice on the program. A masterful showman, he had adroitly leveraged the scandal into a larger stage. After being cut from *Parker & Rene*, he'd distanced himself from the senator and ingratiated himself with leading personalities on the left. After a brief retirement from showbiz to let the scandal fall squarely on Stevens's shoulders, he weighed his options.

When the Clear Air Network offered him a seat, Parker felt it would be good for his image to step into a moderate program that advertised its fairness, balance, and support for free speech. He could maintain his stances while distancing himself from the scandal's more viral moments.

While an intern wired his mic, he picked up his cue cards. "Ironic," he noted as he sifted through the sheets.

"What?" Sam asked.

Parker chuckled. "Our lead story."

"*Thought* you'd appreciate it." Sam grinned. "Looking forward to your take on it."

"You'll have it momentarily.," Parker smiled back.

"May the best man win," Sam tossed back good naturedly.

Parker nodded.

"Places!" the producer shouted from behind the cameras. "We're on in thirty."

Interns darted from their positions as the hosts squared themselves up to face the cameras. The logo animation and bold intro music flashed across dozens of monitors as the red light on Camera Two flashed. The last echoes of the narrator fell silent as the title card faded to a close-up of Claire.

"This is *Pan-America*—the show where *you* get respect and *free speech* gets airtime. With me tonight are Sam Flint, our voice on the conservative side of the table, and Parker Fleming, our brand-new voice for the liberal side. And I'm Claire Mendez." Claire turned to Parker and smiled warmly. "Welcome to the show, Parker."

"Thank you, Claire." Parker's deep, soothing voice swam over the airwaves. "I'm glad to be here."

"We're excited to have your contribution on controversial topics that concern our viewers—and we're starting out tonight with the heat dialed up!" Claire announced.

"That's right, Claire," Sam said. "Tonight is election night, and as results filter in, we're looking at some very heated key races across the country. One state race in particular has America sweating, and it happens to be a special election runoff in Parker's home state."

Sam glanced Parker's way, and the highly polished showman picked up the ball like it was a pinpoint pass. "That's right,

Sam. This race is for the open seat of former Senator George Stevens," Parker explained, reading the teleprompter almost subconsciously, "and it's nuclear-hot tonight. Both opponents have been running neck and neck the entire campaign, and with more than half of the precincts reporting in, the race is still too close to call. The hot-button issue in this race is the fate of the Universal Women's Healthcare Act."

"That's right," Sam added. "The conservative front-runner, Arnold Forscythe, has vowed to repeal the act, while the liberal front-runner, Bill Harris, vowed not only to keep it in place but to *extend* the provisions of the act, despite the corruption controversies surrounding it that lead to Stevens's resignation. And if Forscythe is successful, this election could doom several similar bills across the country."

"Parker," Claire noted, "you have some inside information about this race, right?"

"I do. Senator Stevens stepped down amid allegations of corruption. He was the primary sponsor of the act, and his scandal significantly eroded support for the provision. In fact, following revelations of Stevens's corruption, the bill passed by just a *single vote* in the State Senate."

"Some opponents," Sam interjected, "including myself, believe that the bill was passed illegally, and if the seat is snapped up by Forscythe, the state legislature will have the votes to pull it down. The gubernatorial candidate for the state rode this scandal to a six-point lead over his opponent, so if the legislature brings it, he'll sign it."

"Usually, once a bill like the Universal Women's Healthcare Act is passed," Claire asked, "scandals like this don't lead to their repeal. Why is it different this time?"

This was a perfect moment for Parker to shine.

"The exposé by teen author Mercy Patterson, Senator Stevens's *own granddaughter*, had a *huge* impact on voter opinion. Voters have begun to believe that clinics are not as safe as advertised. Worse, Senator Stevens's treatment of his granddaughter made him seem like a monster to the voting public, and that perception got tied to the headline work Stevens had poured his life into. His own constituents demanded his resignation, and several key swing votes in the legislature jumped ship."

"And," Sam added, "if Stevens's party can't clinch this seat tonight, the Universal Women's Healthcare Act is a goner—and I for one would like to see it go."

"That would be sad," Parker shot back. "It would be unfortunate if the foolishness of a single power-hungry man would cost thousands of women quality healthcare."

"But wasn't Mercy's testimony electrifyingly clear?" Sam countered. "Despite its name, the act offers no material value in terms of *actual* healthcare. I mean, provisions like those in S. 1344, such as a four million in cash windfall put *directly* into the hands of abortion mill practitioners like Dr. Morris, the abortionist presiding over Bridgett Matthews's fatal abortion— while *eliminating* liability for medical negligence in the event a girl like Bridget *is* harmed during the course of an abortion. These provisions aren't just unconscionable—a case can be made that they are *unconstitutional* as well.

"Throughout the bill, special interests got careful attention, while absolutely nothing was covered in terms of real healthcare for women—*except* unlimited access to abortions at *all* stages of pregnancy, up to and including moments before a full-term, natural birth, and this act uses *state money* to pay for them. The Universal Women's Healthcare Act was simply a personal cash-cow for Senator Stevens."

"And on that note," Claire interjected, "we have a new round of election results. More rural districts are reporting in, and we're seeing an interesting trend in the Forscythe-Harris race."

The results chart wiped onto the screen, showing photos of the two candidates next to a percentage estimate of their votes.

"While both ran neck and neck in the metro areas," Claire continued, "Forscythe has taken a solid lead in the rural districts. Some report a spread of over ten percent, giving the conservative candidate a statewide edge of nearly four percent at the polls. Given the trend, I think we have a good idea of who will come out on top. With just twenty percent of districts left to report, over three-quarters of which are rural, we might be getting onto firm-enough ground to call this race."

One viewer watched the TV with keen interest. A little toasted and rather frustrated, he was poring dismally over election returns. He seemed rather disheveled and depressed. A fifth of bourbon sat beside him on the end table, and his shot glass stayed busy.

It was Senator Stevens.

Former Senator, that is. In the wake of the scandal, his party had not only forced him to resign, they had practically disowned him. The opposing party launched an investigation and pushed the state attorney general to file criminal charges. His colleagues didn't offer a peep in protest.

During tonight's special election, he was forbidden from showing himself, lest he mar the chances for the new party pick. He was even disinvited from the victory celebration. Hanging at home, keeping company with only himself, he eagerly watched the votes stack up.

Going into the election, polls had given his candidate a three-point lead. It was a tight squeeze, but it looked like they'd pull off a win. But as votes poured in, the playing field seemed to have shifted—and Stevens was sweating.

The phone rang. Stevens picked up. "What!"

He glanced up. The TV screen showed that 85 percent of the districts had reported in, and the anchors were calling the election. The lead was tight, but with only small rural districts not reporting, the results were pretty solid, and the four-point lead was enough to hold on.

"Are you seeing the reports?"

The voice on the other end was deep and low. Stevens stiffened and flushed as he realized who was on the other end. There was an edge of sinister fury behind the quiet comment.

"It looks like the opposition candidate took the seat," the caller continued.

"Don't worry," Stevens urged. "I'll fix this. I've got a—"

The man interrupted. "I had high hopes for you. Suddenly you are no longer useful."

A soft click left Stevens stunned.

He slammed the phone down. It was over. He chucked his shot of bourbon at the TV. Liquor shot everywhere, and the small glass projectile shattered his TV screen.

The nightmare had only just begun.

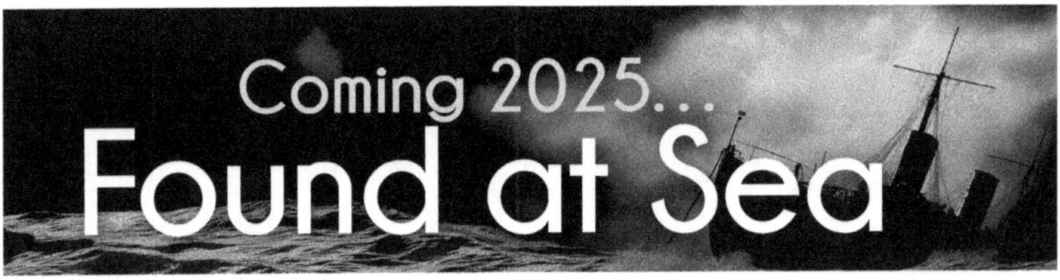

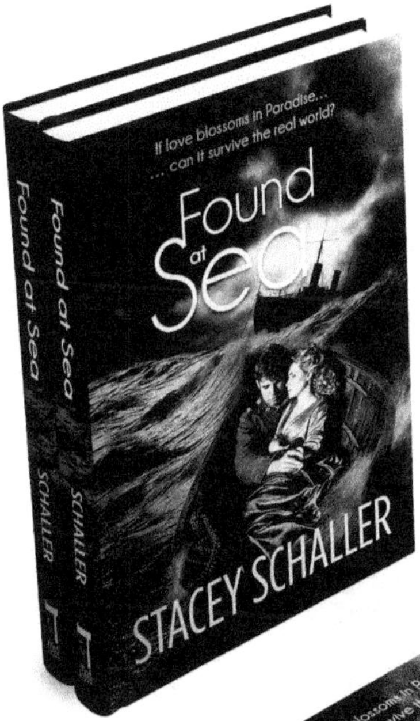

If love blossoms in Paradise...
... can it survive the real world?

She's a princess, born to power and privilege. He's a veteran, recovering from the ravages of war.

She's destined to be queen over a vast industrial empire. He's marching toward life as a missionary in the jungle.

Now, they're shipwrecked — alone on a desert island... and they don't even like each other.

Follow the link below for a free Sample Chapter

ldodipress.com/live/product/found-at-sea/

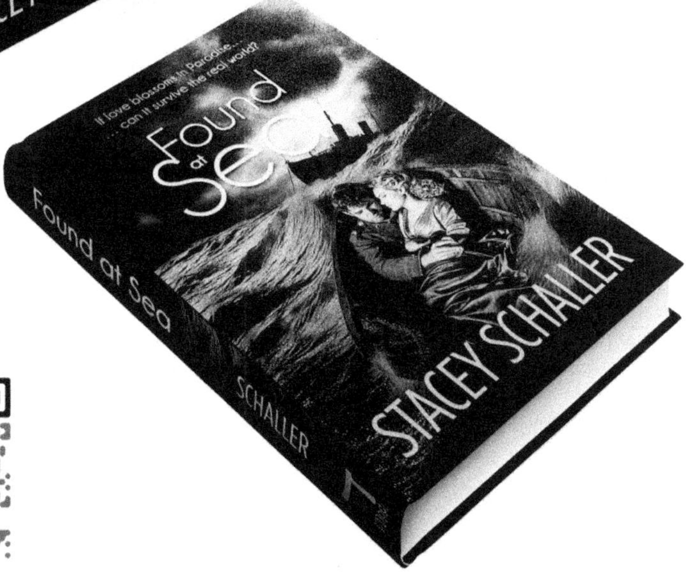

For Every Person that Reads the Book...
10 are Waiting for the MOVIE
an
Angel's
Blood
THREE WOMEN
TWO CAUSES
ONE SHOCKING
SECRET
CHOOSE
LIFE
HELP US PRODUCE IT
Visit: angelsblood.sbs/go/movie.php